If Maxton would just give the world a ch  n
better. He coul
This instan
did the fact tha
Explosion intac

I wonder how. Had the Universe spared him for her? Was that why she felt so incredibly light-headed in his presence?

MF smiled politely as Maxton rambled on about a group of explorers who'd once wandered near his lair. They'd been looking for the Fountain of Youth.

"I tied them all to trees and made each watch as I dragged their intestines from their belly buttons. It was very entertaining."

MF chuckled politely. "I'll bet." *Please look at me. Please open your eyes. I'm way more interesting than your stupid torture stories.* "You know what I think, Maxton? Not that we know each other well, but I think you'd really benefit from blowing this pop stand. There's a whole new world outside this jungle, waiting for you. And if you wanted some company, you could, oh, I don't know, consider starting your own family?"

"Family?"

"Yeah. You know? You, the master, plus an adorable female subordinate." MF patted a pigtail. "Perhaps you'd like a few wayward love-sucking demons who enjoy traveling, too?"

"A coven? With pets? Never. I am a solitary creature." He huffed.

"I just think if you took the time to—"

"This is where we must part ways." He stopped and looked down his nose at her.

"Sorry?"

He pointed to a line of stones cutting across the path. "This is where my territory begins."

"Oh." She blinked. "Are you saying I'm not welcome?"

Suddenly, the ground shook. *Wow. That's a new vampire power.* "Are you serious?"

"No one is permitted within the boundaries of my lair. Unless they wish to die. Do you wish to die, MF? Because I assure you it will be a violent, slow, and painful death."

Her mouth flapped for a moment. How could he be so open and friendly one moment and then ice cold the next? "But I thought that—"

"You thought wrong. Now, I must make haste to my cave. The sunlight is draining my energy." He bowed his head. "Goodbye, MF."

She stood there, her mind spinning as she noticed the muscles working on his angular jaw, almost as if he were thinking about chewing something.

Me? Does he want to drink me? She didn't get the impression it would be the fun kind of drinking either. He wanted to kill her.

The ground shook again.

OTHER WORKS BY MIMI JEAN PAMFILOFF

COMING SOON!

Draco ← Ooh ah! King's son!

Mr. All Out of Love (RevoLUVtion #3) ← Last book?

She's Got the Time (M.O. Mack, Suite #45 Series) ← Still stuck.

The Immortal Tailor, #3 ← Title TBD

THE ACCIDENTALLY YOURS SERIES

(Paranormal Romance/Humor)

Accidentally in Love with…a God? (Book 1)

Accidentally Married to…a Vampire? (Book 2)

Sun God Seeks…Surrogate? (Book 3)

Accidentally…Evil? (Novella, Book 3.5)

Vampires Need Not…Apply? (Book 4)

Accidentally…Cimil? (Novella, Book 4.5)

Accidentally…Over? (Book 5, Finale)

THE BOYFRIEND COLLECTOR DUET

(New Adult/Suspense)

The Boyfriend Collector, Part 1

The Boyfriend Collector, Part 2

FANGED LOVE

(Standalone/Paranormal/Humor)

THE FATE BOOK DUET

(New Adult/Humor)

Fate Book

Fate Book Two

Mack (Book 4)
Ten Club (Book 5)
The Dead King (Book 6)
Lord King (Book 7)
Never King's (Book 8, Finale)

THE LIBRARIAN'S VAMPIRE ASSISTANT
(Standalones/Mystery/Humor)
The Librarian's Vampire Assistant (Book 1)
The Librarian's Vampire Assistant (Book 2)
The Librarian's Vampire Assistant (Book 3)
The Librarian's Vampire Assistant (Book 4)
The Librarian's Vampire Assistant (Book 5)
Vampire Man (Book 6, Finale)

THE MERMEN TRILOGY
(Dark Fantasy/Suspense)
Mermen (Book 1)
MerMadmen (Book 2)
MerCiless (Book 3)

MR. ROOK'S ISLAND TRILOGY
(Contemporary/Suspense)
Mr. Rook (Book 1)
Pawn (Book 2)
Check (Book 3)

THE OHELLNO SERIES
(Standalones/New Adult/Romantic Comedy)
Smart Tass (Book 1)
Oh Henry (Book 2)
Digging A Hole (Book 3)

Battle of the Bulge (Book 4)
My Pen is Huge (Book 5)
Wine Hard, Baby (Book 6)
Baby, Please (Book 7)
Two Sticky Nuts (Book 8)

REVOLUVTION SERIES
(Romance/Action/Dark Humor)
Mr. Ultra Mega Love (Book 1)
Just Mr. Love (Book 2)
Mr. All Out of Love (Book 3) ← Coming soon!

SUITE #45 SERIES by M.O. MACK
(Thriller/Suspense/Action)
She's Got the Guns (Book 1)
She's Got the Money (Book 2)
She's Got the Time (Book 3) ← Coming soon-ish???

WALL MEN TRILOGY
(Dark Suspense/Paranormal)
A Haunted House (Book 1)
A Vow Broken (Book 2)
A Promise Kept (Book 3)

WISH, a Standalone Novel
(Romantic Comedy)

VAMPIRE IN THE JUNGLE

THE IMMORTAL TAILOR SERIES
BOOK TWO

MIMI JEAN PAMFILOFF

A Mimi Boutique Novel

Cover Design: Sweet 'N Spicy Designs
Developmental Editing: Stephanie Elliot
Copyediting and Proof Reading: Pauline Nolet
Formatting: Paul Salvette

WARNING

This book contains a deadly immortal tailor, a rage demon, a bottle-humping sex fairy, a hot vampire in a very hot jungle, violence, bugs, corny humor, strange steamy moments between unattractive immortal creatures, steamy moments between attractive immortal creatures, crazy gods, and some whining.

If you do not like deadly immortal tailors, rage demons, bottle-humping sex fairies, hot vampires in very hot jungles, violence, bugs, corny humor, strange steamy moments between unattractive immortal creatures, steamy moments between attractive immortal creatures, crazy gods, and whining, then this book isn't for you.

VAMPIRE IN THE JUNGLE

CHAPTER ONE

Damien Greystone willed himself not to strangle the redhead bathing in a tub of grape jelly. But he'd be a fool to think he could go up against her, a powerful goddess.

As things stood, the insane deity had him by the balls, and with this power, she'd been slowly turning his life into a circus.

Her latest stunt was the last straw. *Completely unforgivable!*

"Cimil." He stared at the bubble machine to his side, avoiding her nakedness. "I understand you are all-powerful and all-knowing; however, you have brought back the *only* two women I have ever cared for from the dead. Willa was a witch and not a kind one. She will eat Sky alive." And Sky, being a modern woman, would not stand for being threatened, degraded, or pushed aside. In short, this was a disaster in the making. *What the devil was Cimil thinking?*

"You're welcome!" Cimil declared triumphantly.

No. Not welcome. "What I do not understand,"

he brushed off the bubbles accumulating on the front of his navy suit, "is why you would then force them *both* to work for me." Cimil had told the women that if they wanted to get back inside living bodies, they each had to sidekick for him.

"Don't think that just because you're all," she waved a hand in his direction, "smokin' hot with pouty sex lips, that whining will work on me."

He was *not* whining. And his looks were irrelevant, though she wasn't wrong. He was an exceptionally handsome man—tall, physically fit, thick brown hair like all Greystone men.

"Cimil, I am not above using my looks to my advantage when the situation calls for it, but today is *not* one of those days. I do not need sidekicks. Especially those two women."

She inhaled deeply and blew out a breath, sending more bubbles in his direction. "Damien, you are my right hand now—my sheriff—the scrum to my scrumdiddlyumptious plan. That makes these lovely ladies your deputy scrums. But alas, you are right. Having both around will only cause distraction. Therefore, you may choose one."

"Oh, thank you," he said dryly. "That is going to sit well with the ladies." Cimil was loving this, wasn't she? But that was Cimil. She wasn't happy if she wasn't creating chaos (and then coming to the rescue so she could be the hero). Unfortunately, her solutions always came with a price.

Case in point, he had agreed to be Cimil's right

hand in order to bring back Sky—the woman he accidentally ran over with his SUV. He also happened to find Sky insanely attractive. Why wouldn't he agree to Cimil's terms?

Little did he know that Cimil would also bring back Willa, his first love from almost two hundred years ago. To be clear, that relationship had not ended well.

"I choose neither," he replied, "because we both know that anyone who gets close to me miraculously ends up dead."

Going to whine about me now, brother? You are such a pussy. Some people have three, four, even five souls inhabiting them. You, though? Just one extra. And he's awesome. You're also welcome.

Damien ignored the evil twin residing inside him—an inherited trait like his thick dark hair. All Greystone males were born this way. And yes, the twins were always psychotic, murdering assholes.

"Then lucky you," Cimil said chirpily, "because you get to pick whichever woman you want to keep close." Her smile melted away, replaced by a savage gleam in her turquoise eyes—a sign of her divinity. He now had the same color eyes, compliments of Cimil, who had demanded he accept her gift of immortality. He guessed it was to make him a little sturdier for the dangerous tasks ahead.

"And if I do not choose?" Damien folded his arms over his chest.

"Then I will kill them both instead of one."

His stomach lurched. "You-you want to *kill* the woman I do not choose?"

"Yes siree, Bob. And just to make it interesting, I will *also* kill both women if you fail your next mission. *Comprende?*"

"You cannot do this."

"Can. Have. Done. And now you must leave. You're disturbing my purpling. My man, Roberto, will be home soon, and this is his kinky surprise." She leaned forward, whispering, "He loves the corpse look. See you back here in one week. You'd best get that fine tailored ass of yours on a plane to Brazil."

"Brazil?"

"Hellooo? Remember? The last living vampire?" Cimil scooped a bunch of jelly in her hands and smeared it on her face. "He was last spotted hiding in the rainforest. You must find him and convince the hermit-ified vampire to come out of hiding. Bring him here to me. We have a lot of work to do, restarting the entire vampire race."

A few years ago, most of the supernatural life on the planet had been wiped out in the Great Explosion. Any creatures that were once human, such as vampires, became human again. The other creatures simply died, though a handful survived for unknown reasons. In any case, the event prompted the gods to retire shortly after. With so few supernatural creatures left alive, it seemed like the perfect time to pursue other interests and allow humans to fend for themselves. Now Cimil was secretly breaking her retirement and meddling everywhere, including this next mission to have Damien find the last living vampire.

"Cimil," Damien said, "you once told me he wants nothing to do with the modern world. Why would I, a man who completely sympathizes, disturb him? Clearly he wishes to be alone."

Cimil narrowed her eyes. "Because I told you to. Now shoo! Shoo with your shoes. You have one week."

One week? Fucking goddess. Damien turned to leave and then stopped. "Cimil, there will be a day when this relationship of ours comes to an end. I will not do your evil bidding forever." The question was, how could he get out from under her thumb?

"We shall see, tailor. We shall see."

He headed for the door, fuming. The gods-damned goddess was taking things too far. He could never choose between Willa and Sky. Yet that was to be his reward for a successful mission? Let one live. Let one die again.

He had to find a way out of this.

Almost to the door, he stopped and turned. "The rainforest is a vast place. Where do I start looking for this vampire?"

"Pay Brutus a visit. He can help."

Brutus? The deadly immortal soldier who once served in the gods' army? This was going to be a joy.

CHAPTER TWO

"No, Pet. Out." Damien plucked the tiny lavender fairy from the front pocket of his backpack and set her on the bed, where he was organizing his gear.

"And *I* already told *you*; where you go, I go. It's not safe for me here."

Damien narrowed his eyes at Pet. "In this house, there is nothing to fear except you annoying me."

"Someone's in a cranky mood." Pet stuck out her tongue. "And that's not true; there are bad, bad people out there who want to capture me."

"No one knows you're here." Damien looked down.

No Pet.

"Pet?" He opened the front pocket of the backpack.

Empty.

"Pet, I will find you eventually. There are only so many places a pipsqueak can hide in there."

The inner pocket, containing his rolled-up socks, jostled. He reached in and grabbed her, instantly feeling a set of sharp teeth sink into his thumb.

"Ouch!" He pulled his hand away, but the tiny fairy was latched on. "Stop that! Let go."

"No untew you tsay yes," she mumbled with her mouth on his thumb.

Dear gods, he was wasting valuable time and would miss his flight if she kept this up. "Fine. You can come, but no drama, no humping random objects—especially in public—and absolutely no using my toothbrush as a sex toy." Odd that he had to call out such things, but Pet was a sex fairy. Her entire being revolved around behaving like a little pervert.

Pet released his thumb and stood on his immaculately pressed travel suit. "Can I use your hairbrush?"

Damien growled with a stern look.

"Fine," she conceded with solemn eyes, "I'll behave."

"Good. Now let's hurry. I want to swing by the shop on the way to the airport. I have to make sure MF is set to run things on her own while I am away."

"You didn't invite her?" Pet asked.

"Why would I? Time is of the essence, and I will get the task done faster if I go it alone." Besides, only a man such as himself could truly understand and persuade this jungle vampire to come out of the shadows. Damien knew what it was like to revel in one's solitude.

Never alone, tailor.

"Don't remind me, you evil beast," Damien grumbled. What he wouldn't give to truly have his life to himself. But as things stood, he had to be content with only having Pet as his tagalong. She was easy enough to ignore. His twin as well.

"No. Absolutely not." Damien glared down at the two Chihuahuas—one white, one brown—both with big golden eyes, wearing tiny fanny packs. "You are not coming with me."

"Try to stop us," said Bonbon, the white one. He had been squatting here for years at Greystone and Sons, Damien's fine gentlemen's clothing and tailoring shop, but Gorgonzolina was a new edition. And there wasn't a chance in hell Damien would allow either to join him. Both "dogs" were love-sucking demons, and though loyal to Damien, demons like these were needy, always wanting to be held. Sure, it was their form of sustenance, but it was time consuming, not to mention annoying. *All that fur on my suits.* And now, there were two of them. *Thank you, Cimil.*

Like Damien had mentioned, her solutions always came with a price. He'd asked her to find a mate for Bonbon so that the creature could go off into the world and live out its life with a companion. Cimil had delivered on her promise—Gorgonzolina—but with the added bonus that neither demon wanted to vacate his shop.

Damien rubbed his forehead. "Fuck me. My life is so complicated."

"Yep," said Bonbon. "But so is everyone's. Get over it, tailor."

Agreed, tailor. You should spend more time killing. Less time complaining.

"Okay. I'm all ready to go!" MF came from the back room, holding a duffel bag and wearing leather short-shorts, knee-high pleather boots, and a fishnet turtleneck. No bra. She had her auburn hair up in pigtails with studded hairpins on her temples.

Why must she try my patience with her aggressive fashion?

MF was the new manager at his shop, also compliments of Cimil, who felt Damien would need someone to look after things while he was away. Turned out that MF, short for Mountain Flower, had been raised by hippy parents who taught her to sew. She was quite the seamstress.

Ah, but remember how there was always a catch? MF was no different.

MF was an ex-vampire, her vampirism wiped out in the Great Explosion. Her biggest wish was to become a vampire again.

"Absolutely not," he said to MF. "Someone needs to take care of the customers."

MF stared defiantly with her big brown eyes.

"Cimil said my entire future hinges on being turned again, and the only way to make that happen is to convince this vampire to do it."

Damien growled, "Your vampirism is *not* the priority here. It's retrieving the damned vampire. You will simply have to wait to speak to him when he gets here. *If* he gets here."

MF snarled.

"No." Damien put his foot down. "You cannot come. You'll only slow me down."

CHAPTER THREE

"So what do you know about this Brutus guy?" MF asked from the seat beside him, sipping on her inflight cocktail.

Damien snarled in her general direction.

"I don't think he's talking to you right now, MF." Bonbon howled from the dog carrier at his feet. "Damien is a sore loser."

"Oh! I think I understood Bonbon!" MF crouched toward the dog and whispered loudly over the roaring engines, "You said Damien is a giant stuffy prick, right, Bonbon?"

Bonbon and Gorgonzolina snickered. Pet cackled in Damien's jacket pocket.

"Very funny." Damien sipped his whisky.

MF shrugged. "I have my moments. But I'm getting better at this whole love-sucking demon speak."

"They just talk backwards and add the words 'hug me' to the end of every sentence," Pet called out.

Damien pressed his hand over his pocket. "Silence. Someone will hear you."

"Thanks for the tip, Pet." MF turned to Damien. "So tell me about this Brutus. Do you think he's really going to help us?"

"I do not know," he replied. "I've only met the man a handful of times, and he does not speak much. He's Uchben."

"Uchben? Wow. I've never met one before. Is it true what they say? Can they kill you with one look?"

"I think their deadliness has been exaggerated." The Uchben were an organization of mostly humans, overseen by the gods. Their sole purpose was to act as the gods' eyes and ears. Many were soldiers, but others were civil servants, conducting surveillance or doing scientific research. There were even accountants to manage the gods' assets. Brutus was once a highly decorated soldier but retired after finding his mate—some Amazonian warrior princess. Her village was their destination.

"Nevertheless," Damien added, "you would be smart to mind your Ps and Qs around Brutus. He is not the sort of man you wish to make angry. Nor his mate. I hear her tribe is very savage."

MF waved a hand through the air. "If I can handle Big Foot, I can handle anyone."

"So he stopped urinating on your doorstep?" MF had insulted the creature one day when he came into the shop for new slacks.

"Not yet, but I can tell my offerings are starting

to have an effect. Yesterday, he only pissed on half the door. He seems to like Luna Bars."

Damien shook his head. "Just do me a favor, and do not provoke anyone. Let me do the talking."

MF nodded, clearly mulling on something. "Boss?"

"Yes?"

"What are you going to do about Sky and Willa?"

"I do not know," he replied.

"Where're they now?"

"I also do not know." It had been a few days since he'd seen them for the first time in their new bodies. Neither woman looked the same, but he could recognize their anger anywhere. Once they learned that Cimil had brought them back so that they could *both* be his partners, they stormed off. *Just wait until they find out about Cimil's new terms.*

Or maybe best not to tell them? Damien had no way of getting a hold of either one anyway, though Sky did have a sister and nephew. It was possible that Sky had gone to seek them out.

"It is a good thing they are not here," he said. "It will allow me time to think with a clear head."

"Well, you know you can't work with both of them, right?" MF said. "That would be a disaster— your most recent fling versus your pregnant ex-lover who died at the hand of her abusive husband because you refused to rescue her?"

"Who told you that?" he snapped.

"Cimil mentioned something. Is it true?"

Yes. One hundred percent. You are a bad man, tailor, and so am I. Two peas in a pod.

"Shut the fuck up," Damien snapped at the beast.

"Jeez. Sorry." MF held up her hands.

"I was speaking to…never mind. It is not true. Not entirely. So drop it." The truth was that Willa had been a witch with great ambition, so she married a duke. And yes, Damien had slept with her afterwards. And gotten her pregnant.

Damien hadn't been opposed to running off together, but she'd had other plans. Mostly, murdering her husband and having Damien pretend to be the duke's long-lost brother, a brother who stood to inherit all the land and titles.

Damien had wanted no part of it, so they went their separate ways. Her husband had ended up poisoning her after suspecting the baby in her belly did not belong to him. It was a tragedy Damien blamed himself for despite Willa's role. He should have taken greater measures to protect her.

As for Sky, she'd died because he had been distracted by an annoying sex fairy—Pet—who lodged herself in his nose while he was backing up his SUV. He ran over Sky. *Poor, poor woman. Looked like a pancake. I'm a monster.* Even worse, they fooled around after she became a ghost. And he liked it.

"Do you still love Willa?" MF asked.

"I love no one," Damien grumbled.

"Liar. I know you love Sky."

"If you recall, I ejected Sky from my life the moment I made the deal with Cimil to have Sky brought back to life."

"Ah, but you did that out of concern, because you still believe anyone you care about dies."

It's true, his beast said. *We are a wonderful death sentence. MF knows. She's seen me in action. Maybe someday I'll get to slit her throat while you watch, brother.*

Damien snarled, "You are *not* touching her."

"What?" MF asked.

"Nothing."

"Your beast is talking shit about me, isn't he?" MF asked. "Well, if you're listening, creepy parasite, you should know you don't scare me. You're just a dark shadow clinging to Damien's light because you know you're worthless without him. And that makes you a big fat nothing of a coward."

I am going to remove your lips and tongue, MF, and sew them to your eyes so you can taste the horror I rain down upon your soul, starting with disembowel—

"Enough, you two. I need to think," Damien growled.

"Fine, but he started it." MF folded her arms over her chest.

"Pretend my brother does not exist, as I do, MF. And be thankful you cannot hear him."

"Doesn't make him any less of a sick fuck."

True. And MF would know. She'd recently witnessed his brother's handiwork at a dinner party.

The beast had broken through Damien's control, only to kill the host's entire family, the staff, and security. Unfortunately, most of the victims were members of the Russian mob. Also unfortunate, someone had taken photos and mailed them to the shop. No note.

What did they want? Probably money. Damien would have to deal with that later, but it was just one more example of why it was essential to stay in control and keep those he cared for at a distance. His twin was always waiting in the wings, eager for that moment when Damien let his guard down.

"So which woman are you going to pick?" MF asked.

"I do not know. Nor will I have to worry about it if I do not convince this vampire to return to civilization. Cimil has promised to kill them both if I fail."

"She did what?" MF's jaw slacked.

"I will lose them both all over again if I do not locate this vampire and persuade him to return home with me. If I succeed, she will only kill one."

MF covered her mouth with a gasp. "I'm so sorry, Damien. I didn't know. That's really messed up."

He nodded in agreement.

"Well, then, lucky thing you brought your posse."

He slowly turned his head. "Yes. So very lucky. What could possibly go wrong with you four by my side?"

CHAPTER FOUR

Sky Morales stared into the rearview mirror of the black Jaguar she'd "borrowed" from Damien's house without his knowledge.

What could she say? He wasn't home when she swung by, and he had garages filled with cars. It was difficult coming back to life, especially in the unfamiliar body of a woman with no ID, no money, and no credit card to rent a car.

Sky fixed her long honey blonde hair and studied her emerald green eyes. *So damned weird.* She'd been born with dark hair and brown eyes. And a big ass. *I liked my big ass.* This body had more of an athletic look. Lean, tall, strong. Tight small ass.

Be grateful, she told herself. *Because it could've gone the other way.* Cimil was the sadistic type, so Sky wouldn't have been surprised to end up in a body with a bad ticker, nonstop flatulence, and missing teeth. All in all, Sky felt pretty lucky.

Sky exited the car, heading for the motel lobby. *Please be here. Please be here.* Sky had already checked fifteen small motels along the coast. Her sister, Amelia, had said she was taking Sky's nephew, Miguel, to the beach for a few weeks but never said which one. Nor was she sharing her life online these days.

Why? Long story, but before Sky's unfortunate death, she had been a freelance journalist and published several investigatory pieces on a sex-trafficking ring. The ring turned out to be much more than that. In any case, there were people in high places who hadn't wanted the story to go public.

For Amelia's and Miguel's safety, they'd gone into hiding.

Now Sky wasn't sure what to do. Officially, Sky was dead. The threat was over. On the other hand, she had no intention of staying quiet or not releasing the rest of the story as originally planned. The world needed to know what the governor and his wealthy friends were up to.

Sky trudged toward the motel lobby and spotted Amelia entering a room at the far end, carrying bottles of water.

Oh, thank God! Sky's heart squeezed in her chest. How she'd missed them—their hugs, her sister's laugh, Miguel's feistiness, the weekend barbeques. The three of them were inseparable.

Sky knocked on the door.

"Who is it?" Amelia said from the other side.

"I'll give you three guesses, but here's a hint: you threatened to kill me if I left, even though I was a ghost." After Sky had died, her soul stayed put in this world, anchored to Damien.

Why? She didn't know, but their relationship eventually cascaded into a whirlwind romance. Her first love. Only to be rejected.

Imagine that. A ghost falling in love with the living. They'd even had ghost sex a few times. Very hot. So when Cimil had offered to bring her back to life, Sky thought it meant being with Damien for real. But no. He said he couldn't risk harming her due to his whole evil-twin situation.

It hurt. It truly did. And to make matters worse, it turned out the Cimil had decided to bring back Damien's first love, too. *What the hell, Cimil? What the hell?*

The door flew open, and Amelia stared up. "No. Is it? Did you? It worked?"

Sky nodded. "It's really me."

"I don't believe it." Amelia covered her mouth. "You don't look anything like my sister."

"When I was eight, I took your favorite doll, Princess Bakes-a-Lot, without asking, and when you tried to take her back, we fought. You hit me in the eyebrow with her tiny frying pan, and blood went everywhere. Left a small scar, too. Not that I have it anymore." Sky pointed to her right brow.

"Ohmygod. It's you. Sky!" She flung herself into Sky's arms.

৵ ৵

"I'm sorry about how we fought last time," Amelia said as they walked along the beach, where Miguel played in the waves, splashing and diving. It was good to see him acting like a kid after everything they'd been through—upping and leaving their home, his aunt dying and coming back as a ghost. And then returning as a blonde in a new body. Very weird.

"I understand why you were worried," Sky said, "but I felt like I didn't have much to lose. Being a ghost is no fun."

"Yeah, but you were really amazing at it. The way you drove cars and mastered a cell phone. Pretty cool."

Cimil had helped her learn a few tricks. But little did Sky know, everything Cimil did came with a price.

"So? How do you feel?" Amelia asked. "I mean, wow. That's quite a new shell you've got."

"I don't know." Sky sighed. "Part of me is disgusted by what those traffickers were doing—torturing all those supernatural creatures to harvest stem cells. On the other hand, they figured out how to grow new immortal bodies with all that stuff." Sky was here in a new body because of them, sort of a lemonade situation.

Cimil had told Sky that the main lab for SBP (Supernatural Body Parts) was going to be burned to the ground. It wouldn't stop their gruesome work, but it would slow them down for a while.

Either way, their facilities had had two new bodies ready for new owners. Cimil had offered one to Sky.

"Don't let those creatures die in vain," Cimil had said and then assured Sky that the body would feel like a regular human, though at the cellular level, it was something entirely different. Shifter, fairy, goblin, and whatever else SBP used for stem cells. What did that make Sky? Hell if she knew.

"I'm glad to have you back," Amelia said. "Even if you look like Malibu Barbie."

Sky looked down at her chest. "A little flat for Barbie, but I'm glad to be back, too."

"So, do you know what you'll do next?" Amelia asked.

"That's what I want to talk about. I have to work for Damien. It's part of the deal." Something Sky fully intended to get out of. No way would she work side by side with the man she loved and Willa. Sky had seen the way he looked at Willa after being brought back. He still loved her.

"Okay. And?" Amelia asked.

"I want to take down the governor and all his rich friends who backed SBP and trafficked those women." They were being used as test subjects. Then there were the poor creatures who'd been carved up like tiny turkeys while still alive.

"You want to pick up where you left off with the story?" Amelia asked.

"Yes." Sky didn't want to let this second chance be wasted.

"But what about Miguel and me? They think you're dead, but if you start publishing again, they'll think I'm behind it, using your notes or something."

Amelia was right. "What if I can come up with a way to remove you from the situation completely?"

"I'm listening."

"Just promise that no matter what happens, you won't tell Damien."

"I don't talk to the man, but why would you be worried?" Amelia asked.

"He's not going to like what I'm planning."

CHAPTER FIVE

"Could it be any hotter?" MF groaned, swatting at the hundreds of grape-sized mosquitoes following her through the jungle. They seemed to be intrigued by her scent, but not enough to go in for a taste.

It probably had something to do with the fact that after the Great Explosion, her body hadn't returned to its former human self. She was no longer a vampire, but some of her immortal traits remained: eyesight and hearing, for example. Damien's hypothesis was that the explosion didn't kill the vampire side of her DNA, it merely made it dormant.

Truthfully, he found it all very interesting, especially the fact that there were pockets of supernatural creatures who were completely untouched by the blast. Pet for example. Bonbon and Gorgonzolina, too. He'd even met a pack of were-eagles recently. Why had they been spared?

Also a mystery? How does anyone survive in this sticky heat? Dear gods, it's hot. He'd even had to change from his casual business wear to a white linen shirt and khaki linen shorts. He never wore them unless at the beach, but thankfully he'd come prepared.

Almost.

For three days, Damien and his unwelcome posse had followed a game trail through the dense jungle, going up one ravine and down another, through forests so dense that the sunlight could not penetrate. Not that there was any sunlight. The constant rain seemed to follow them everywhere. His balls felt like spent wads of chewing gum.

Now one day's journey had turned into three because they'd been walking in circles. *Never let a demon be in charge of the GPS,* he thought. Their dark energy throws everything off.

"I love this weather," said Bonbon, trotting behind Gorgonzolina, sniffing her brown tail. "Reminds me of home. Kind of like Gorgonzolina's butthole."

"Did they just say hell smells like a butthole?" MF asked, marching behind Damien with Pet on her shoulder.

"Pretty much," Damien replied. "Pet, why don't you fly ahead and see if there's any sign of the village? If I go by my GPS, we cannot be far."

They were less than a mile from the coordinates of where Brutus liked to have his clothing drop-shipped. Generally, Brutus ordered camo cargo pants with extra room in the front, back, thighs— pretty much everywhere. Brutus was a large man.

And this said a lot coming from Damien, who was no small potato at six three with the body of a man who once killed for a living.

"No," MF protested, "I'll go. The last time you asked Pet to scout, she found a mushroom patch and had a one-fairy orgy."

"Fair point." It had taken them two hours to find her, and when they did, it was a sight that no living—or dead—creature should see. "Who knew sex fairies had so much capacity in their orifices."

"I once fucked a donkey," Pet said proudly. "In the butt."

"You had sex with it, or the other way around?" MF asked, her face contorting with disgust.

"Both," Pet replied.

"Ew!" MF brushed Pet off her shoulder. "Did you just leave a wet mark on me?"

"Sorry. I got all excited thinking about Señor Donkey-Ho-Tee." Pet fluttered ahead, landing on Gorgonzolina's back to ride her like a horse.

"This is exactly why I wish to travel alone rather than with you degenerates," Damien grumbled. "This is a serious mission. Not some camp jamboree for perverts and idiots."

"Watch who you call an idiot," MF protested. "And I'll point out that I can out-sew you any day of the week. Blindfolded. Also, *I* wouldn't have forgotten the water back at the last camp." MF fanned her face. "And before you offer again, Bonbon, no, I don't want to drink your demon urine."

"Who goes there!" barked a loud female voice.

Damien stopped in his tracks, his eyes scanning the surrounding jungle. He saw no one. "Everyone, please allow me to do the talking," he whispered.

"I want to see Brutus!" Pet called out. "I hear he is sexy, and I would like to tickle his balls!"

"Pet! I told you not to speak." Damien inhaled slowly. "No one is here to tickle anyone's balls. We've come to *speak* to Brutus!"

"Is that a sex fairy?" asked another female voice.

"Ohmygod. I think it is," answered another.

"What is your name?" one of them called out.

"I am Damien Greystone. I am Brutus's tailor, and I—"

"No, we meant the fairy," said one of the females.

Pet fluttered toward the voices, disappearing into the thick jungle. "Hi! I'm Petra! Oh. Aren't you large sexy women? Can I have a lick?"

Giggles broke out.

"She's adorable," said one woman.

MF and Damien exchanged glances. MF shrugged.

"Please, if I may?" Damien called out. "We were sent by Cimil to speak to Brutus. It is very urgent."

A tall topless woman with dark dreads down to her ankles stepped out of the foliage, wearing only a suede sarong. "Brutus is unavailable."

"Uh, when will he be available?" Damien asked.

"We've traveled a long way to see him."

A blonde stepped out. "It is mating time. Our leader is ovulating. So it could take up to five minutes." The two burst out laughing. "Men. So eager with their lovemaking. Like little rabbits. It's no wonder we spend so much on batteries."

I like these women. They sound like sluts, said the beast. *Let me out to enjoy them.*

Damien pushed back with his mind, feeling his brother growing restless.

"Come," said the first woman, "you may wait for Brutus outside the daycare."

"Daycare?" Damien asked.

༺ ༻

MF looked at Damien, her dark brows scrunched together as they watched several burly Uchben warriors systematically handing off babies to extremely tall, fierce-looking women.

It seemed that the men were feeding, changing, and assisting with the napping, and then handing the little ones back to the mothers.

"This is very strange," Damien muttered.

"Damien?" Brutus appeared in his custom camo pants and a black T-shirt, bouncing a baby with dark hair on his hip.

"Brutus, it is good to see you." Damien shook Brutus's free hand. "But what is all this?"

"Ah, you mean the daddy daycare? My mate,

Fina, is the leader of this all-female tribe. Of course, after I met her, she got pregnant almost immediately, as did her one hundred sisters, whom I also impregnated. Long story."

"I *like* it here!" Pet said.

Brutus continued, "Obviously, one hundred baby boys are a lot of work, so I called in my Uchben brothers to assist. We run the daycare. The women take care of hunting and security."

"I *really* like it here." Pet flew in a tiny celebratory circle.

"So, what can I do for you, tailor?" Brutus asked. "You're a long way from home."

Damien had known this man for years, yet Brutus had just spoken more words in one minute than in all that time. "Cimil sent me. I am here to find a vampire who lives nearby."

Brutus blinked. "You mean Maxton, that old killjoy who lives up there?" He pointed to a waterfall high up on the mountain overlooking the village.

"The vampire lives there?" Damien asked.

"Yes. But if you've come all this way to see him, you're out of luck." Brutus chuckled.

"Why?" Damien asked.

"Maxton sees no one. And if anyone sees him, it's the last thing they see."

"What does that mean?" MF asked. "I'm MF, by the way."

Brutus nodded. "As in Motherfucker?"

"*What* about the vampire?" Damien prodded

impatiently. The clock was ticking. They'd already burned up one day flying and three days hiking here. That left three days to get the vampire back to Cimil.

"Have you ever read the book about the Grinch?" Brutus asked. "Well, try to visualize him. Except that anyone who attempts to speak to, look at, or come within one hundred yards of his lair is never seen again. Not alive anyway. Maxton always leaves behind a little warning for anyone else who attempts to disturb him."

"Warning?" MF asked.

"He enjoys turning them inside out. Imagine a sock. But it's a person."

Damien made a sour face.

Brutus went on, "Best you stay clear of Maxton, tailor. Fina's people have attempted to capture him many times, and it always ends in tragedy."

"Why would they want to kill him?" Damien asked.

"Not kill."

"Then what?" Damien asked.

"Up until our arrival, males have been very scarce in this area. Mostly because the women would eat them—a big dating deterrent."

"So the women hunted the vampire for...sex?" MF asked.

Brutus shrugged. "It was before Fina's time as ruler, but yes. And if you don't want to be sucked nearly dry but left alive so you feel every second of your skin being peeled from your bones, then I suggest you leave the man alone." Brutus lowered his voice. "He's—how should I say—a fucking asshole."

"Did someone say asshole?" Pet clapped. "I like those! When does the licking start?"

"Pet!" Damien barked and then looked at Brutus. "I appreciate the warning. Truly, I do; however, Cimil is demanding I find this Maxton and convince him to come out of hiding."

"She wants him to make more vampires, doesn't she?" Brutus asked.

"How did you guess?" Damien asked.

"Take the worst possible idea ever, and you'll find one of Cimil's hairbrained schemes."

"Agreed." Damien threaded his fingers through his damp hair. "But if your mate's life was in the crosshairs, what would you suggest? How do I speak to him?"

Brutus kissed the top of his baby's head and flipped the infant on to his broad chest, rocking the little man to sleep instantly.

Impressive.

"I have no advice, tailor. The vampire is not a creature who embraces change, which includes his solitary life. Hell, he still wears an ascot, so I hear."

"Did you just say he likes ascots?" Damien smiled.

CHAPTER SIX

"Damien! You heard Brutus. This vampire doesn't want to be spoken to or looked at, let alone dressed." MF closed the door to their guest hut, complete with a baby hammock for Bonbon and Gorgonzolina, where the two swung together while Pet pushed.

In just an hour, they were to attend a special dinner in their honor. That gave Damien just enough time to have Pet fly up the hill and leave the ascot for the vampire—a little warming-up gift.

Damien looked down at MF, who sat on the primitive, straw-mat bed. "Do you or don't you want to become a vampire again?"

"Of course I do, but let's face it; if Cimil says it's my destiny, she probably has some self-serving angle."

"I cannot argue with your assessment. But there is still the fact that it is what you want. Yes?"

MF huffed and then nodded reluctantly.

He added, "There is also the fact that Cimil will kill both Sky and Willa if I do not deliver the vampire in three days."

Not that he needed MF's approval, but it did him no good to go without it either. This mission was difficult enough without having to listen to his team—errr…the idiots who followed him—whining all the time.

He went on, "I will have Pet drop this note and my offering outside the vampire's lair. She will be in no danger if she does as I say." Pet had been instructed to fly fifty feet above the entrance to the vampire's cave and then release the package. The vampire wouldn't even know she was there.

"I don't like it." MF shook her head.

"We don't either, man," Bonbon said, licking his tiny furry balls swinging back and forth.

"Must you?" Damien winced.

"Must *you* keep asking that question?" Bonbon replied.

Damien zipped up his backpack beside MF on the bed. "If anyone else has a better idea, let me know. If not, shut the hell up."

"Give him your Armani," Gorgonzolina piped up. "If you really want to win him over, go all in."

"I'm not giving him my emergency travel Armani," Damien protested. "That suit cost fifteen thousand dollars, not to mention the custom tailoring, mother-of-pearl cufflinks I found specifically to match that shade of black, and the gray scarf made from four-week-old angora rabbits, woven by an old woman with the softest, most dexterous

fingers known to man. The ensemble is priceless."
Also, he never went anywhere without a spare suit.
One would be surprised how often they came in
handy.

Pet, MF, and the two demons stared with contempt.

Why the fuck was everyone glaring at him?
They knew he loved his suits. Just like he loved
convertible automobiles, the wind in his thick hair,
expensive scotch, and cheap Chinese food. A man
needed his comforts, not because he was fussy, but
because he was immortal and needed something to
look forward to.

MF stared, her eyes flinching with disapproval.
"Do you or don't you love Willa and Sky?"

"I love no one. I never have. I never will."

*God damn, tailor. You are so pathetic. Not willing
to kill. Not willing to love. Not willing to give up your
travel suit. Stand for something, brother. Anything. Or
move the hell over and let me drive. Because I fuck-
inguaranteeyou, I'll stand. I'll slice, chop, choke, and
butcher, too. Five in one, baby!*

Damien drew a slow breath. They were all gang-
ing up, attempting to emotionally manipulate him.

But here were the facts: that ascot was silk. One
of a kind. Dyed with Pompeian ash spewed in 79
AD. It was said that when the fabric shimmered in
the moonlight, you could see your death. He'd
never witnessed such a thing, but any gentleman
worth his salt would know that the ascot was the

finest this world had to offer.

If Damien gave up his suit now, along with the ascot, what would be left to bargain with? A sex fairy, two smelly Chihuahuas, and an ex-vampire?

"I will throw in my travel scarf just so he knows I mean business," Damien said, pulling it from his backpack. "But the suit stays here as a possible bargaining chip." He rolled the note inside the ascot and scarf and handed them to Pet. "Pet, I mean it. You go, you drop, you return. No detours to mushroom patches, no stopping to make out with tropical flowers because they remind you of vaginas, and absolutely no talking to that vampire. Got it? Because if you fail, it will cost Sky her life. You like Sky. She's your friend, remember?"

Pet nodded.

"Good. Off you go." He opened the hut's door, and Pet fluttered off.

"What was in the note?" MF asked.

"The truth."

"You told him Cimil's going to murder your two exes?" Bonbon asked.

"Yes. Also, if he did not help me, and they died because of it, I would personally invest in building an amusement park on his doorstep. Also, I offered him some new suits if he came to LA."

"Do you think this is going to work?" MF asked.

"All the man must do is visit Cimil, make a few vampires, and then he can return to his cave. What is there to think about?"

Of course, there was only one issue: Damien had no clue why the vampire was hiding out in the jungle to begin with. Made bargaining a little difficult.

తా తా

"So is it normal that the men eat alone?" Damien asked as Brutus turned the wild boar roasting on a spit over a large fire. Meanwhile, the women were up the hill, gathered around a massive bonfire, eating their dinner.

"Trust me," Brutus said, "you don't want to get anywhere near them when they eat. They turn feral."

The other ex-soldiers around the fire nodded in agreement.

"Are you…happy here, Brutus?" MF asked.

"Compared to working for the gods and dealing with their shenanigans every day, this is heaven. And after a lifetime of fighting and killing Maaskab, evil vampires, stupid humans, and whatever else the Uchben were tasked with, I am more than happy to just kick back and let the women do it. I get to play with my son, teach him sword fighting, weaving, fishing, welding—once he's old enough, of course. And my men enjoy around-the-clock sex because there are three women to every man."

"Hear, hear!" said one of the soldiers.

"Hear, hear," the others roared.

Brutus leaned in to whisper, "Plus, I really love Fina. The woman has a heart of gold, and she's always down for a good romp."

"Did someone say romp?" Pet appeared in front of Damien's face, holding a piece of paper.

"Pet, what happened?" Damien asked. She'd been gone for over forty minutes.

Pet handed Damien the note. "I had to wait while he wrote a reply."

"You spoke to Maxton?" Damien growled.

"Didn't you say to read him the note?" Pet asked.

For fuck's sake, she's even dumber than Bonbon, said the beast.

Damien shook his head and unrolled the note, which was written on the back of the paper he'd sent. A foul odor hit his nose. "Is that…shit?" Damien held the note away from his face.

"Yup. That's what took so long. He went out, found some squirrel turds, and then carefully wrote each word with a broken femur he had lying around."

"What's it say?" Brutus asked.

"*Fuck your women. Fuck you. Fuck off. Come near me, and I will slice off your dick and make you eat it.*" Damien frowned. "*P.S. Thanks for the ascot and scarf. You have excellent taste. Cheers.*"

I like him! the beast roared.

"Silence, brother. You are not helping."

What? I am merely thrilled to learn I have a true brother out in the world.

"Who are you talking to?" Brutus asked, looking around for a hidden stranger.

"Damien has a psychotic twin living inside him," MF said. "He kills people any chance he gets."

The Uchben traded glances.

"I am in control of him. There is nothing to fear," Damien said. "He merely talks a good game."

"Not true. I saw him slaughter an entire dinner party. Took him ten minutes," MF interjected.

CHAPTER SEVEN

"Thanks, MF. This is just what we needed. Now we'll have to eat granola bars for dinner again." Damien jabbed at the tiny campfire with his stick and glanced across the wide river at the village, the smell of Brutus's roasting meat making his mouth water. Reminded him of a good moo shu pork.

"Well, maybe Brutus had a point to unwelcome us," MF said. "They have a hundred babies to think about, and you're a wild card."

Perhaps. Either way, they had not gone to the village for its accommodations. They'd only needed to learn the whereabouts of Maxton.

"So what's the plan now?" Bonbon asked, standing with Gorgonzolina, the two rubbing their butt cheeks together.

"Stop that," Damien snarled. "I'm trying to think." What was the plan? They didn't have much time left. "The vampire seemed to appreciate the ascot and scarf, so fine. Send him the suit." Maybe it would buy a little goodwill.

֍ ֍

The next morning, Damien woke to campfire smoke in his face. He rubbed his eyes and the back of his stiff neck.

I must've been tired, he thought. He'd slept in the dirt and hadn't woken once through the night. *Oh crap. Pet!* She'd gone to leave the suit last night.

He looked over to find her snuggled between Bonbon's furry legs.

He got up and grabbed her by the wings, dangling the sleepy creature in front of his nose. "Pet! Wake up! What happened? What did the vampire say when you gave him the Armani?"

Pet rubbed her tiny eyes. "He said he's coming for you now, so you'd better prepare."

"Coming for me?" Damien arched a brow.

"Yeah," she replied. "He said he'll take out the entire village too. Babies and all."

I love this guy! The beast chuckled. *He's very entertaining.*

"Was he serious?" Damien asked Pet.

Pet nodded. "Oh yes. He said he was, and I quote, 'going to enjoy tearing every last one of you to pieces while wearing his new suit. He seemed to really like it, by the way. Fit like a glove. Then he walked off and started sharpening spears."

Damien's stomach rolled. "We cannot allow him to do this."

"What's happening?" MF asked, sitting up now,

swatting at the bugs still lurking over her. "Dammit. I can't wait to be a vampire again."

Damien looked at her, a deep sadness filling his heart. "Maxton is coming to kill us and the entire village." He swallowed hard. "I must stop him."

"What!" MF stood. "You're going to fight him?"

"I will attempt to subdue him, but if that is not possible…" His voice trailed off. Killing the vampire was the last thing he wanted. It meant going home empty-handed.

"You'll lose Willa and Sky. I won't become a vampire," MF protested.

"I know." But what else could he do? He'd brought the wrath of this insane vampire upon this sort-of-peaceful village filled with children. And mothers. And oddly whipped, but happy ex-warriors. "They did not ask for this, and I must do what is right."

Yeah, now we're talking, tailor. Let me at him!

"MF," Damien added, "I need you to cross the bridge and tell Brutus what has happened. Warn them. If I fail to stop Maxton, then the vampire will be knocking on their huts, and they must be prepared."

MF shook her head, glancing over her shoulder at the female warriors on the other side of the river, guarding the small wooden bridge.

"Do not worry, MF. They will not harm you," Damien said.

"I'm actually wondering what it would take to

join their village." She snapped a furious gaze his way.

"I am sorry, MF. Truly," Damien said. "Take Bonbon and Gorgonzola with you. You'll all be safer over there."

"What about Pet?" MF asked.

"Pet can keep everyone informed. If I lose the fight, it means I'm dead." Even if he had the light of the gods, his body could be destroyed. He could still die. "In which case, you may want to consider running."

CHAPTER EIGHT

Dressed in his hiking boots, black linen slacks, and his last fresh linen shirt, Damien made his way up the steep path leading to the top of the waterfall. Pet hovered nearby, humming and singing as if he were part of a musical performance for the demented.

"He's going to kill. Kill, kill, kill the vampire! I'm going to watch. Watch, watch, watch! This is so much fun. Fun, fun, fun…"

Make her stop, or I will kill, kill, kill her first while she watches, watches, watches.

"Pet, stop singing," Damien barked.

Thank you, tailor. By the way, before we arrive, you and I need to have a little chat.

"What about?"

You think that just because I love killing, you can just pull me out, have me murder at the snap of your fingers, and then put me away again?

"So you're saying you do not want to take out this vampire?" Damien highly doubted it.

I'm saying that I want something in return for doing your dirty work.

"What?"

I want one week a month to do whatever the fuck I want. Eat, kill, kill some more, fuck. Whatever.

"Not a chance." The beast would just run out to the nearest mall and slaughter indiscriminately, leaving Damien holding the bag.

You believe that I cannot control myself, that I will go on a rampage.

"Yes."

But is it also true that if I decided to do such a thing, you could easily take back over.

"I suppose."

So then, if I promise not to kill, and I break our deal, you could return to keeping me at bay.

"Are you saying that you agree not to kill anyone?" Damien tried not to laugh.

Only one way to find out.

The beast had a point. Damien was the stronger one. He could always take over. The only problem was that in that brief amount of time it took to overpower the beast, the beast could take out dozens of people.

"I'll have to think about it."

Sure. But I'm not fighting that vampire until you agree.

"Then I don't agree. So I guess I'll just have to fight the vampire on my own."

"Damien!" Pet called out from above. "Something's coming your way."

But they weren't anywhere near the top.

"It's him!" Pet called out. "Yoo-hoo. Maxton!" She waved.

Damien could see the brush and vines moving up ahead.

Changing your mind about my offer, tailor?

"No. I can take him," Damien said, though in his heart, he wasn't so sure. Fact was he'd likely have to kill this vampire, and that meant the deaths of Willa and Sky. How would he ever explain this to them or forgive himself for failing these women yet again? They deserved better. They deserved happiness and long lives.

But I can take him faster.

"Forget it. I'm not letting you out one week a month."

Fine, one weekend a month.

The vampire drew closer.

"One weekend a year," Damien countered.

Fine. Deal.

"Fine. Deal."

Now let me out, brother. Let me show this smug sonofabitch who is the true king of the jungle.

Damien closed his eyes, inhaled slowly, and relaxed his mind, opening the cage where the beast lived.

Like a shock to the system, Damien felt his twin flow through his veins, filling his muscles, organs, and skin. Meanwhile, Damien shrank into a place in his own mind where he could see, feel, and hear everything while his brother drove.

Suddenly, a tall figure with shoulder-length dark hair appeared up ahead on the path. He wore the ascot, scarf, and the fine Armani suit.

The man actually looked great.

"Maxton the vampire, I presume," growled the beast.

"Damien Greystone the tailor, I presume." The vampire's bright green eyes glowed in the shadows.

"Afraid not, vampire."

"Then who are you?" Maxton asked.

"I am the one who is going to bathe in your blood, tear out your organs, and make your balls into a charm I shall wear around my neck. All while you remain awake. I hear from the locals, that's the way you do business, yes?"

Beast! You must try to subdue him first! Damien roared.

"It has been a long time since I've enjoyed a fair fight. Bring it on, tailor."

"I already said I'm not the tailor. I am your executioner." The beast charged.

Beast! Subdue! Damien tried to force the beast back into the cage, but the fight was already on.

ᢙ ᢗ

Late in the afternoon, Damien woke by the side of the raging river, Brutus staring down with a grin. "Looks like someone had fun."

Damien glanced at his naked body covered in

mud, blood, and bits of leaves. "What happened?" The last thing he remembered, the beast had the vampire in a headlock and the two were rolling down the steep mountain toward the waterfall. Then they went over. He distinctly recalled screaming his lungs out as they fell hundreds of feet toward a cluster of boulders below.

"You and that vampire went at it for hours," Brutus said.

"Went…at…it?" Damien questioned, sitting up and rubbing the huge knot at the back of his head.

"Not that way, tailor. You fought nonstop for hours. The ladies even got out the popcorn and chairs. It was quite the spectacle." Brutus scratched the side of his head. "Never seen anything like it."

MF ran up, panting. "Oh good! He finally found you! Damien. Ohmygod. That was amazing! I've never seen anyone take so many punches. And, wow, the way you dished right back? How are your balls, by the way?"

"What are you talking about?" Damien looked down at his penis and then covered it with his hand. Thankfully, everything looked intact.

"Don't you remember?" MF asked.

"No." And it was highly unusual. Had he blacked out after the waterfall while his beast stayed conscious?

Damien reached into his mind, feeling around for his brother. He was asleep. Passed out, actually. *What the hell?*

"Either way, tailor," said Brutus, "you have earned some serious respect from Fina and her sisters. There's talk of a statue."

"Where's the vampire now?" Damien stood up, feeling like his body had been run over by several semis. And a herd of elephants.

"He's in my hut." Brutus chuckled. "You know, I think you were just what he needed to bring him out of his shell. Damned vampire won't stop chatting."

"You are joking, yes?" Damien asked.

"Come see for yourself."

CHAPTER NINE

MF and Brutus entered the large hut ahead of Damien, who decided to stay outside listening—just to be on the safe side—as the vampire reminisced with some of the villagers about the good old days, when he used to truly enjoy being a vampire.

"Killing had meaning. It felt powerful yet challenging to take a life," Maxton said.

"It's not anymore?" asked MF, sounding a little peppier than usual.

"When I was a new vampire, I never knew the outcome before I hunted my prey. I mean, yes, I could overpower any mortal, but there was a piece of my soul that struggled and questioned every kill. Sometimes, I walked away out of guilt. Other times, I overcame my moral objections and took the life. The point is that the outcome was never predetermined. Even if I hunted a depraved murderer, rapist, or child molester, which were always my favorites to dine on, there were moments when I said to myself, 'Maxton, why not simply break his legs and arms and throw him in a ditch? Allow him to suffer.'"

"So why did you run off to hide in the jungle?" someone asked. Damien couldn't see who.

"One day, I woke up, and it was gone. I no longer cared who I killed. If I came across any immortals who challenged me, I was old enough to overcome them." Maxton sighed. "Life just didn't have meaning anymore."

Holy hell. Was this vampire saying he got bored of being a vampire? That was why he was here in this jungle? Damien shook his head. Sounded a little pathetic.

Maxton went on, "So I wandered the globe, searching for meaning, and do you know what I found?"

"What?" Brutus asked.

"Nothing. Absolutely nothing except the desire to die."

"Why didn't you?" MF asked.

"Suicide? Never. I am a Catholic."

Damien blinked. *Huh? Suicide no, but killing innocent people yes?*

Maxton continued, "So here I remain, hoping that someday a creature strong enough, brave enough, will find me and end my life. Last night was the closest I've come. A great fight, but not enough to do the job."

He just got lucky, Damien thought, stepping inside the crowded hut. "Hello, vampire."

Maxton sat in the corner on a wooden chair, his

dark hair combed neatly back. He wore only a white dress shirt covered in mud. No pants, no shoes, nothing else. He was surrounded by eight warrior women, who stared with lustful fascination, plus MF and Brutus.

"Beast." Maxton dipped his head, his green eyes vigilant.

"The beast is napping. I am Damien Greystone. Pleasure."

"Did you forget your clothing?" Maxton asked.

Damien looked down at his nude body. "Yes, well, I do not know what happened to my clothes, and someone has my emergency travel suit."

Brutus handed Damien a pair of leather pants. "Here. I can't wear these anymore. Much too hot for this weather."

"Gee. Thanks." Damien snatched the pants from his hand and slid them on. Yes. They were very hot. And they smelled of sweaty balls. Also, they had been stretched out to Brutus's shape. On Damien, they looked like a deflated leather balloon.

MF giggled. "Someone needs to work out more."

"I beg to differ," said Maxton, rubbing his jaw. "That body packs quite the punch. And I would return your suit, but I'm afraid it was ruined during our fight."

So that was why Maxton was only wearing a dress shirt. *Can't believe he killed my suit.*

Damien held back his anger. "I can always get

another," he lied. It was no longer produced by Armani. "What I am concerned with is you coming back to LA with me."

"That's what we were chatting about earlier while Brutus was out looking for you," said MF. "Maxton has vowed never to leave this jungle."

"Because you're tired of killing?" Damien asked.

"No. Because I am a vampire who finds no joy in his purpose. My life has no meaning."

"Because you're tired of killing," Damien repeated.

"Exactly," Maxton replied.

Alrighty, Damien thought.

"I get it. I do," Brutus said, standing beside MF. "There comes a point where you start asking yourself, why? I kill, I kill, then I kill again. But does it change the world? Does evil cease to exist? No. So then you ask, well, is there anything in it for me? Any sense of satisfaction or pleasure? No."

"You understand me well, Brutus." Maxton bowed his head.

"I hate to break up this bromance," Damien said, "but there is an insane goddess who doesn't care if you enjoy killing, being a vampire, or if you've taken a vow. She will kill the only two women I have ever lo—sworn to protect, and they are more important than your feelings of vampiric impotence."

"Damien, did you not hear the man?" MF snapped. "He doesn't want to go."

Suck-up. She was just agreeing with Maxton so that he might give her his blood.

"I do not see the point of breaking my vow." Maxton raised his chin smugly. "If I go to this place you call LA, it changes nothing. The world will continue spinning in one mundane circle after another."

Damien growled.

"Damien, can I speak to you outside?" Brutus asked.

Damien nodded, and the two walked down the hill a ways, stopping under a large tree filled with Amazonian suede panties.

"Laundry day." Brutus shrugged.

"What is it you want to say before I take that vampire, tie him up, and drag his ass back to LA?" Damien grumbled.

"You won't make it, tailor," Brutus said. "I watched him fight your beast for hours. You are evenly matched. Also, there isn't sufficient time to walk to the nearest airport."

"I'll run."

"Or you could listen to my suggestion. I will fly you in our helicopter to the nearest Uchben airstrip and personally take you to LA. I need to make a diaper run at Costco anyway."

"You have a helicopter? And a plane?" Damien asked.

"Of course. You don't expect us to live out in the middle of the jungle without proper transportation? As for the vampire, I sense he is lying."

"About?" Damien asked.

"I have fought in many wars. I have led many soldiers into battle against some of the fiercest creatures the Universe has to offer, and I have seen this situation before. I believe Maxton did not grow bored of killing, he grew to enjoy the violence too much. He lost control, and this is what upsets him. Anyone can see he is a rigid creature with a predilection for boundaries. And what are boundaries but a form of rules. He likes discipline. Control."

Could Brutus be right?

Because now that Damien thought about it, Maxton's story did not sound right. New vampires loved killing. Small or large. Young or old. Day or night. They just couldn't get enough. As they got older, their bloodlust quelled, and they became more focused on their legacies. That, or power and wealth. Either way, vampires felt a sense of relief when they were no longer controlled by bloodlust.

But then there were those who never lost the taste. Killing was an addiction that controlled every aspect of their lives.

It was exactly the reason Damien had left behind his life of violence. There came a day when he no longer knew where his beast ended and he began. He became sickened by himself—the monster is a fine suit, controlled by a wickedness inside him.

So, one day, he quit cold turkey, shut the door on his beast, and pushed everyone away. His tiny shop became his sanctuary of control. He worked alone. He focused his days on keeping busy and doing something familiar, something he'd been doing since he was a boy working in his father's shop. He made suits, and he tailored.

"He savagely murders anyone who gets near his lair," Damien muttered. "It's because he can't stop himself. He created rules, and when anyone breaks them, he loses it. So why is he here in your hut, just chitchatting away?"

"I do not know, but look at the man. He almost seems, well, free. Or relieved. Something or someone here is causing it." Brutus stared at Damien poignantly.

"You mean me?" Damien pointed to himself.

"Maxton could not best your beast."

Of course not. Yawn... What did I miss, tailor?

Damien pondered for a moment. "He's free because he has someone to keep him in check," Damien muttered. "He's not afraid of killing indiscriminately."

"It's just a hypothesis, but if I'm right," Brutus shrugged, "then you might be able to convince Maxton it is safe to leave the jungle as long as he's with you."

"But what if you're wrong, Brutus? What if he still won't agree to leave the jungle?"

"Did Cimil specifically say you had to deliver him alive?" Brutus asked.

Yes! And the fun begins. I'd love to finish the job,

tailor. Let me out! Let me kill him!

"She did not." And while Damien did not wish to kill Maxton, the vampire no longer wished to live anyway, so what would be the harm? Win-win all around.

"Then I suggest you exploit that loophole and do whatever it takes to earn his trust," Brutus said. "You'll need it to convince Maxton to go with you, or you'll need it to blindside him and go in for the kill."

Damien could see why Brutus was known for winning battles. He had ruthless instincts. "Please do not tell any of this to my team."

"As you wish, but your assistant is already smitten with him. She has barely left Maxton's side since he regained consciousness. She even went around and collected blood to revive him."

Well, fucking great. Add to the pressure. "Thank you, Brutus. I appreciate your advice. I will have a chat with our vampire friend."

"You do that, though Fina has requested you return to your side of the river. She doesn't want you around the children."

"What about the vampire?" Damien arched a brow.

"He's not an outsider with a beast living inside him. He is welcome as long as he behaves."

"He's killed your villagers," Damien pointed out.

"That was long ago and only because they violated his privacy. What can I say? There are many dangerous creatures in this unspoiled corner of the world, and Fina's people believe in living in harmony with them."

"How progressive," Damien said dryly.

"MF and your demons are welcome here, too, but not the sex fairy. She keeps humping the women's sword hilts, like a tiny horny dog. It's disturbing."

"Try living with her. She keeps ruining my scotch. Leaves little slug trails all over the bottle necks."

Brutus winced. "You keep company with strange creatures, Damien. But I'm not surprised. You, yourself, are a strange creature."

Brutus walked away, leaving Damien to think. He was a strange creature, wasn't he? He'd always considered his beast separate from himself—just a genetic anomaly experienced by all the males in his family. But when it came down to it, Damien was a freak of nature. *And I think I can use it to get the vampire to trust me. Birds of a feather and all that.*

CHAPTER TEN

Wearing camo overalls, Willa watched from behind a large stand of passion fruit trees as Brutus and Damien discussed convincing some vampire named Maxton to go back to LA. That or killing the poor sod.

Very interesting! Now I know why Damien's here. Willa had been watching him since the group departed LA. None of them noticed her, of course, because when it came to cloaking herself, she had her tricks.

Her new body had straight black hair and rather voluptuous lips along with a generous bosom. But with the snap of a finger, she could appear blonde, short, and old. Or invisible.

Yep. Still got it. After two hundred years of being dead, she hadn't forgotten a thing. And thank goodness for that, because she desperately wanted to find out how Damien felt.

Did he still love her?

Did he want her by his side again?

Because if he was leaning toward Sky, she'd have

to make sure he changed his mind. *With a little help.*

That was the other thing she was good at: love spells. It had worked once on Damien, and it would work again.

Yes, yes. She was a dirty bitch of a witch. *So what?* People who played nice never got ahead in life, and she wasn't about to lose the perfect man— dedicated, smart, and the kind of handsome that only came around once in a blue moon. Of course, the thing she loved most about Damien was his deadly nature.

A true weapon for a woman like me to have in her arsenal. She was not about to lose him to another. This was her second chance at getting everything she'd ever wanted.

First things first, though: Willa had overheard Damien chatting with that MF bitch on the plane about how Cimil had given Damien an ultimatum.

Treacherous goddess! Luckily, I am slier than her! Willa would first ensure Damien brought this vampire back to LA. Then Damien would choose her, of course. After, he would help her build the empire she'd always dreamed of. With herself in charge, of course.

No need to marry dukes or kings in this day and age. Women could own land, run companies, and even have children on their own. No one cared! She was going to have it all: an army of slaves, money, mansions, lovers, and power. And with Damien by her side, she'd crush anyone who got in her way.

First, I will meet with this vampire. I will con-vince him to leave this jungle with Damien.

Willa returned to the village to wait for her op-portunity to get Maxton alone.

MF walked with Maxton up the steep trail leading to his lair high above the mountain. It felt like her insides were about to melt.

He is so hot! From the first moment she saw him, his smoldering jungle-green eyes had punched right through her and sucked the thoughts right from her head. Then there were his beautiful supple lips and shiny dark hair down to his shoulders. He reminded her of a Spanish prince with his deep olive skin and fine features.

I could look at him all day. She sighed, listening to his deep voice. He had just a hint of an accent, like a man who'd seen the world, lived everywhere, but belonged nowhere. He just screamed cultured, educated, and fearless. Also, a little out of step with the world, but she could fix that.

Sigh… What I wouldn't give to spend my life look-ing at him. How was it that this exquisite man had lost the will to live? If only he could get out of his head, he might see what she saw: a world filled with possibilities.

Sure, some things would never change. There would always be taxes, stupid people—very good vampire eats—and not enough hours in the day to sew, read, and chase off creatures who urinated on one's doorstep. But the world had changed a lot since Maxton had gone into hiding centuries ago. Cars, for example. Cars were cool. No more walking for hours or having to get on a horse. With a car you could just hop in and travel long distances or simply run to the store.

Oh, and snacks! Not that he ate solid food, but even he would be amazed by the selection at the store. Mini pizzas, tamales, cheese balls, chocolate-covered nuts and berries.

I think I'm hungry. The food in this village sucked. *Roasted pigs and weird fruit. Bleh.*

And what would Maxton think if he rode in a plane? Or went to an amusement park? Or Damien's shop?

Christ, the mall! So many suits in every fabric and color imaginable! If Maxton would just give the world a chance, she could get to know him better. He could get to know her.

This instant attraction has to mean something. So did the fact that this vampire had survived the Great Explosion intact.

I wonder how. Had the Universe spared him for her? Was that why she felt so incredibly light-headed in his presence?

MF smiled politely as Maxton rambled on about a group of explorers who'd once wandered near his lair. They'd been looking for the Fountain of Youth.

"I tied them all to trees and made each watch as I dragged their intestines from their belly buttons. It was very entertaining."

MF chuckled politely. "I'll bet." *Please look at me. Please open your eyes. I'm way more interesting than your stupid torture stories.* "You know what I think, Maxton? Not that we know each other well, but I think you'd really benefit from blowing this pop stand. There's a whole new world outside this jungle, waiting for you. And if you wanted some company, you could, oh, I don't know, consider starting your own family?"

"Family?"

"Yeah. You know? You, the master, plus an adorable female subordinate." MF patted a pigtail. "Perhaps you'd like a few wayward love-sucking demons who enjoy traveling, too?"

"A coven? With pets? Never. I am a solitary creature." He huffed.

"I just think if you took the time to—"

"This is where we must part ways." He stopped and looked down his nose at her.

"Sorry?"

He pointed to a line of stones cutting across the path. "This is where my territory begins."

"Oh." She blinked. "Are you saying I'm not welcome?"

Suddenly, the ground shook. *Wow. That's a new vampire power.* "Are you serious?"

"No one is permitted within the boundaries of my lair. Unless they wish to die. Do you wish to die, MF? Because I assure you it will be a violent, slow, and painful death."

Her mouth flapped for a moment. How could he be so open and friendly one moment and then ice cold the next? "But I thought that—"

"You thought wrong. Now, I must make haste to my cave. The sunlight is draining my energy." He bowed his head. "Goodbye, MF."

She stood there, her mind spinning as she noticed the muscles working on his angular jaw, almost as if he were thinking about chewing something.

Me? Does he want to drink me? She didn't get the impression it would be the fun kind of drinking either. He wanted to kill her.

The ground shook again.

MF shrank back, holding in her emotions, and walked away. She was never one to cry much. In fact, the last time she'd had a good gusher was after she lost her family to the vampire who turned her. He'd then abandoned her, leaving her alone to figure out what she was.

Sadistic fuck.

A month later, the Great Explosion had happened, and she had been human again. And lost. So lost. Everything she knew—her human life, her family, her humanity, and her vampirism—had been wiped out. She'd ended up on the streets, ready to give up, when Cimil had appeared with an offer.

"You work for the tailor. Help ease his mind so he leaves his shop and does some very important work for me. In return, Mountain Flower, I will see to it that your life is set back on course. A vampire. A purpose. A family."

"You say you're a powerful goddess, so bring back my parents instead. Give me back my old life," MF had said.

"I am sorry, my bitter little cookie," Cimil had replied, "but some things are beyond my control. Except on Wednesdays. And even then, there must be Twinkies. And naked clowns. I am afraid that day isn't today."

It actually had been Wednesday; however, MF immediately understood two things in that moment. One, the goddess wasn't right in the head. And two, this would be a take-it-or-leave-it situation. Cimil had an agenda, and whatever she was offering wasn't negotiable. So MF accepted to serve the tailor. All to become a vampire once again and find her destiny.

But if Maxton wasn't interested in her, there wasn't a chance in hell he'd bite her. In fact, he'd just threatened to kill her.

MF arrived back at the small camp on the opposite side of the river from the village, finding Damien talking to Pet.

"The moment Maxton emerges from his lair at

sunset, I want you to tell me," Damien said.

"Why? Are you going to make out with him?" Pet asked.

"No, Pet. I wish to speak with him."

Pet shrugged, her eyes spotting something off in the distance. "Mushroom!" Pet fluttered away.

"Come back here!" Damien shook his head.

"Hey," MF said glumly, "I'm going to ask Brutus to give me a ride to the Uchben airstrip."

"You're leaving?" Damien cocked a brow. "I thought you wanted to help convince Maxton to go to LA."

"I wanted to convince him to turn me, but that's not going to happen."

Damien's turquoise eyes filled with pity. "Wars are not won in a day, MF. Give him time."

"You have two days to get him back to LA."

"I meant give him until tomorrow. Then we must haul ass home."

"What'll you do if he says no?" she asked.

"I will cross that bridge when I get there. For the moment, I have a few cards up my sleeve. MF, I must ask about something Brutus mentioned. He seems to believe you are romantically interested in Maxton. Is this true?"

Had her drooling been that obvious? *How humiliating.*

"No. I, uh, I think he's handsome, but romance? *Pfft!* Not my thing."

Damien nodded hesitantly. "Very good."

"Why're you asking?"

"Because I may have to kill him to save Sky or Willa."

Her heart plummeted to the floor. "Kill?"

"I know Cimil wants him alive, but Cimil did not stipulate it in our deal. A mistake on her part. So he either comes along willingly, or he comes dead. Makes no difference to me. Unless you are lying, and it matters to you."

Yes, Maxton had flat out rejected her. And maybe threatened to give her a violent death, but she didn't want him to die. "I just think it's better for everyone if he comes willingly."

"But you're okay if he doesn't, yes?" Damien prodded. "It'll mean you won't become a vampire."

Maybe not *now*, but if Damien killed Maxton, that door would be shut forever! On the other hand, was her vampirism more important than Sky's life? MF was convinced Sky was the one for Damien. And who wanted to take away that kind of love from a man who needed it so much?

MF sighed. "Sure, boss. I'll be okay."

Damien patted her on the arm. "You're a good woman, MF. Terrible taste in casual wear, but good nonetheless."

CHAPTER ELEVEN

Kill the vampire? Is Damien mad? Willa thought. Even if Cimil had not been explicit about the terms, no way in hell would that crazy goddess accept a dead vampire on her doorstep. Cimil did not strike her as the sort of woman to appreciate being played either.

I would know. I am a sore loser, too. Also quite manipulative, she thought proudly as she hiked up the mountain with just a few minutes to go until sunset. She needed to put the whammy on the vampire before Damien got there.

She made her way up the steep, slippery path that snaked up the perimeter of the five-hundred-foot waterfall, and stopped just shy of the line of scrimmage: Maxton's boundary. Once she crossed, she'd be fair game, completely reliant on her wits.

Willa drew a breath and stepped over the stones.

"Vampire!" she called out. "I have violated the sanctity of your territory and am approaching your lair. Come out here and face me!"

Willa came around a small bend on the trail and

stopped.

"What are you doing here?" Maxton's eyes were black, like a feral animal.

She smiled and waved her hand. "I have come with an important message, vampire. And you shall listen."

꙳ ꙳

"That went well!" Willa hiked down the trail, feeling very pleased with herself. The vampire had been much easier to bespell than she'd anticipated. Perhaps because he'd worn himself out fighting the beast.

Lucky me. Now all that was left was for Damien to choose her once he got back to LA. Which he would. *Though, maybe I'll put some insurance in place. Then Sky will die, and I'll have Damien all to myself.*

Willa would take out the MF bitch, too, once things settled down a bit. She'd make it seem like an accident. *Vile little ex-vampire. Thinks she has the right to influence my man.*

"Vampire!" Damien's deep voice echoed down on the mountain.

Christ, he is coming this way!

"Maxton, it is I!" Damien called out. "I would have had Pet warn you of my visit, but she is currently engaged with fungi. But I come with important business! Come out and meet me! Or I will come to you, and you will not be spared from my beast this time!"

Willa heard a rustle up the hill behind her, followed by thundering footsteps. *Uh-oh.* She was about to be sandwiched between Maxton and Damien.

She jumped to the side of the trail, hiding behind a cluster of boulders, where she waved a hand over her body. *Hide, hide to all the world. No scent, no heat, no sound to be heard.* Willa's body faded from sight just in time for her to watch Damien march past.

"You have crossed into my territory, tailor," Maxton snarled from somewhere above on the hill. "You know the consequences of your actions."

"Fuck your territory," Damien replied. "If you know what's good for you, you'll listen to what I have to say."

I must see this! Willa carefully stepped back on the trail for a better view of the standoff.

"Are you threatening me?" Maxton chuckled, wearing an old threadbare suit with a ratty ascot. His clothing had to be as old as she was.

"You already know you cannot best me, so why not listen?" Damien proposed.

"My land. My rules. And they do not include indulging in chitchat with my victims."

Damien shook his head with disappointment. "Very well, Maxton. But know that I am here to offer you a new life. Earlier today, you sat peacefully in Brutus's hut. You reminisced about your exploits and kills. You were free for a few short hours from your rules, and I am betting you enjoyed it. I could offer you that every day. I will ensure you have no need for your rules. I will *not* allow you to kill. You have nothing to fear."

Oh turds. Did Damien just imply that Maxton was afraid of leaving his lair? Wrong strategy. All he had to do was ask Maxton to come to LA! She'd already made sure he'd say yes.

Maxton growled. "I can count on one hand all the things I fear. Running out of people to kill, running out of people to torture, and running out of…" He paused. "Actually, that is it. Just the two."

"Maxton, I was once consumed by bloodlust. It ruled every minute of my day like a sick drug. But I was able to break free. Granted, my new vices became fine suits, fine cars, and food that is not particularly healthy, but I found peace, and if you allow me to help, you can find it, too."

"What makes you believe I wish to find peace, tailor? Perhaps I like my life of—"

"Of living like a caveman when I can clearly see you are a gentleman? The thing I am wondering is why you have condemned yourself to living in a damp, hot, muddy cave. I do not believe for one moment it's because you are bored of life. You *did* something. Something that haunts you. This isn't your lair; it's your prison."

Maxton narrowed his green eyes.

Willa drew a breath, watching this all go down.

"What do you know about anything?" Maxton roared.

"I know that vampires don't live in jungles unless they are hiding from something or they really, really, really hate themselves. So which is it? Are you a coward or a glutton for punishment?"

"Grrr…"

"Disagree?" Damien threw back. "Then prove me wrong. Come with me to face the world. Face the goddess demanding to see you."

Ugh! Say "LA," Damien. Say "Come to LA!" Willa thought.

"How about you face your death, tailor?" Maxton charged.

Oh no! Willa was about to run out and block Maxton, but then Damien did something she hadn't expected.

"Take him down, beast. Kill the vampire," Damien said.

"No! Don't do that…" As Willa screamed, she watched Damien transform. Him, but not him. Harder, back straighter, fists tighter, and not a modicum of fear to be found in those turquoise eyes.

The beast charged, meeting Maxton head-on with a blow to the head. Maxton flew back, knocked unconscious.

The beast lost no time jumping over him, ready to smash in Maxton's skull with a rock.

"Wait!" Willa rushed toward the beast, revealing herself. "Don't kill him. I can get him to do whatever you want. Just don't do that."

The beast's eyes turned to a deep red, zeroing in on her. His gaze felt like a paralyzing harpoon to the heart, making it impossible to run. She'd never been so terrified in all her life. Not even when she discovered that her husband had poisoned her. Even then she had not feared death. But this?

"Hello, witch." He smiled.

"Just...let him go," she yammered. "I'll make it worth your while. I can get, uh, Damien to give up control more often or...I don't know, but I'm willing to do whatever it takes."

"Are you now?" He stood and marched toward her, hovering over her like a dark cloud of rage. "I want you." He tugged on the strap of her camo overalls.

"Me?" She stepped back.

"Against that tree. I haven't had a good fuck in a long while, and the tailor, well, he likes it too soft. No fun."

Sex? He wanted sex? *Pfft. What an oaf!* Here she was thinking he'd ask for an organ to nibble on or for her to run off and round up a bunch of Amazonian women to slaughter. *This is too easy.* She'd already had sex with his vessel a number of times. Yes, Damien had been at the helm, but the beast was always there, too. Right behind Damien's eyes, watching hungrily.

So what if he wanted to reverse roles?

She smiled coyly and licked her lips. "Give it to me as hard as you like. Just don't stop until I scream your name." She pointed a finger in his face. "You come before me, you'll regret it, beast."

His wicked smile turned into a lustful gleam. He picked her up by the waist, carried her to a large tree at the side of the trail, and turned her around. "I'm going to make sure you finally know the difference between me and my brother."

"Mmmm…intriguing. Oh, before I forget, when you are done, just ask the vampire to go willingly to LA."

"Ask? I do not ask," snarled the beast.

"Then demand. Just be sure to say LA."

"Whatever. Now hold on, witch."

CHAPTER TWELVE

Cimil was tearing open a bag of marshmallows in the backyard, preparing for a big roast, when Minky suddenly appeared. Or whatever invisible unicorns did.

"Minky, what are you doing back from the jungle so soon?"

Cimil listened to the unicorn frantically squawking about some story involving Damien, Willa, and his beast.

"You can't be serious." Cimil tossed a marshmallow into the firepit. "I think you're making it up. Perhaps all that time you spend with your mate—Mittens the hellhound—and your demon-corn children has warped your unihorn." Minky and Mittens had fallen for one another during the Great Explosion. It was an unnatural pairing, but Cimil had to let the creatures work that out for themselves.

All Cimil cared about was that Minky had come back to work for her. *Best spy ever! Also, best weapon ever.* Minky could get pretty stabby.

"Agreed," Cimil said. "Working for me *is* better than Masturbatory Mondays, Taco Tuesdays, and Whateverthehell Wednesdays. It's everything an evil, magic creature wants in a career—answering to no one, killing whomever you like, lurking in the shadows and invading people's privacy. It's like being in the CIA except we don't pretend to be the good guys."

Cimil nodded at Minky's reply and blew her a kiss. "I get you too, Minkster. Except I'm not following what you just told me. You were spying on Willa in the jungle, and Willa is spying on Damien in the jungle? And now Willa and the beast are gettin' busy against a tree?"

Minky nodded.

"Oh no. Oh no. I did not see that coming. This is not good, Minky."

Cimil listened to Minky's screeches.

"Oh gods. You're right. If the beast got her pregnant, that could throw the entire world for a loop. It could spark a bloodline of earthbound demons!"

Cimil dumped the entire bag of marshmallows into the pit, followed by lighter fluid. *How did I not see this coming? Crapola!* If her brethren learned of this fuckup, she'd be in a major timeout.

It had cost the gods greatly to cleanse the human world of demons and seal off all demon portals into the human world once and for all. Sure, a few innocuous demons remained illegally, such as

Bonbon and Gorgonzolina, but they were never a big deal.

It's the other ones people have to worry about. Some demons could enter a person's body and steal their life. *And nuke codes.* Others loved to hijack your social media and send annoying photos to all your friends. But the worst of the worst were so evil, so violent and powerful, they were capable of busting through the gods' seals on the demon portals.

Rage demons. Cimil shivered in her pink lederhosen.

That was why hundreds of years ago, when the gods had devised a plan to rid the world of demons, step one was to capture the rage demons instead of sending them back to their realm.

But what sort of prison could possibly contain such a powerful beast?

Therein lay the question of all questions. The big greasy enchilada of questions.

It had been Cimil's idea to bind these rage demons inside a human male with a bloodline stronger than the rest. A bloodline known for conquering and never surrendering. The Greystones were an ancient people who loved their gold adornments, fine woven fabrics, and, most importantly, enslaving the most vicious of immortals to do their bidding.

That's right. These rage demons were imprisoned inside hardened warriors known for subduing the most violent creatures.

The assumption was that as these original Greystone men died, the rage demons would die with them. Extinction.

But uh-uh-uh… Not so fast. What Cimil had not anticipated was that the demons would fuse to the human, and when new children came along, they carried the demons' genes like a hitchhiker.

Female children never survived because they weren't big enough assholes. Not the case for the Greystone males, though.

Anywhoodles, it all led to two sets of DNA, two souls sharing one body. The evil prisoner and the jail keeper.

Really, the whole thing was an abomination. One big accident!

Fast-forward to today, and Damien was the last of his kind. With him, the last rage demon would finally die out. I.e., it was never in the cards for Damien to procreate. *Who does he think ratted to Willa's hubby about the baby not being his?* Yes, a dick move, but no one ever said protecting humanity from rage demons was pretty.

Of course, that did not mean that Cimil wouldn't use Damien while he lived. That kind of hotness mixed with intelligence and fighting skills didn't come along often.

But babies? More Greystones with rage demons inside them? *No. Absolutely not.* Cimil had to nip this Willabeast sitch in the bud.

Cimil looked at Minky. "Time to pull the plug,

Minkster. Kill Willa."

Minky howled.

"Yes, yes. I know. The plan was to let Damien discover for himself what a treacherous woman Willa is and that his love was never real—all just a fancy mind trick. That way he'd pick Sky, but Sky wouldn't pick him back, and he'd finally, once and for all, give up on love! Then I'd have the use of his skills until he dies in a glorious volcano mishap." He was immortal, yes, but not Cimil's kind of immortal. Damien could die if his body was destroyed. Kind of like a vampire.

"I hear you, Minky. But you must take out Willa. Make it look like it's the beast's fault or an accident. And yes, you can wait until they're done having sex. I'm not a monster."

Minky flashed away, and Cimil went back to work. "Now, where was I?" Cimil looked down at the man tied up in her backyard firepit.

She'd caught this creep in the bushes at the park, touching himself by the swings while looking at her precious little evil ones.

"Ah, yes." Cimil grabbed a book of matches from her pocket. "I am sorry to inform you, but the Underworld is too good for your kind. You are going straight to hell. Aka, the Underworld's basement." She smiled down at the man lying under a pile of marshmallows.

"Cimil, darling, where are you?" Roberto, her hubby, called from inside the house.

"Just taking out the trash! Be right there!"

Minky suddenly returned, yammering on about something.

"What do you mean 'Willa put the whammy on the vampire, and if she dies, he'll immediately explode'?" Was that even possible? If so, where could she learn that mindfuck? "So I can't kill Willa without losing Maxton?"

Minky neighed.

"It is as if she read my mind and knew what was coming."

Minky added a few other tidbits. Apparently, Willa had also commanded Maxton to come willingly to LA.

"This is good! Great even. We just need Maxton to make a bunch of vampires, starting with my hubby and kiddos, and then we can take out Willa. We won't need her or the vampire anymore."

Minky shrieked.

"Your pious lectures are getting boring, Minky. We can't make everyone happy. MF's heart will heal eventually. She will find a new mate. Someday."

CHAPTER THIRTEEN

"Boss. Boss! You need to wake up. Hurry!" MF jostled Damien's shoulder.

"Jesus, my head." Damien woke the next morning in the moist dirt next to a smoldering campfire. "What happened?" he groaned.

"I don't know, but you have a bigger issue than your noggin." MF looked down at his fully exposed groin.

Damien sighed. "Don't tell me. The beast took over again."

"Whatever he did, you need to thank him because everyone's waiting on you to get to the helicopter. Everyone *including* Maxton." MF clapped excitedly, jumping on the balls of her feet.

Damien sat up slowly, rubbing the back of his stiff neck. "What are you talking about?"

"You did it! Whatever you said to Maxton last night worked. We have just enough time to get to LA to present him to Cimil."

For the life of him, he couldn't remember a thing past giving control over to the beast. "Are you absolutely sure?"

"Yeah, dude. So get your leather pants up. By the way, why are they down?"

Damien stood slowly and pulled up his shame, aka the pants. He loathed wearing clothing that fit improperly. "The beast's idea of a joke, no doubt."

"Don't know anyone who could laugh at that shlong." She grinned. "You got it going on, tailor."

"Thanks," he said dryly. Damien grabbed his things, his head spinning in two different directions. In one direction, he wondered why he kept blacking out. This was not good. It meant he couldn't jump in and take over if the beast was crossing any lines, which he usually did. In the other direction, Damien wondered what the beast had done to sway the vampire.

Regardless, this was the turn of events he'd been hoping for.

Damien righted his leather pants, grabbed his backpack, and crossed the small wooden bridge stretching over the river. One of the women greeted him on the other side.

"Mind your Ps, Mr. Tailor. And your Qs. Or you'll have my S up your A."

Damien blinked. "Sorry?"

She pounded the butt of her spear onto the ground.

"Oh," he said, "that S and my A. If you'll simply point me in the direction of the helicopter, I'll be out of your very lovely long dreadlocks for good."

She pointed her spear downriver. "Ten minutes that way."

Damien turned toward the river.

"Hey, tailor?" the woman called out.

He stopped, looking over his shoulder.

"You make sarongs and baby clothes? We have too much hunting to do to make them ourselves. These men eat a lot."

Suede panties and jungle infant wear? *Sure, why the hell not?* At this point, his suit shop had lost all dignity the moment two tiny demons moved in. "I am sure we can arrange something to suit your needs."

Damien headed for the helicopter, grateful that his time in this sticky, wet jungle was over. But somehow he suspected this had been the easiest part.

෨ ෧

MF couldn't believe her luck! That big, gorgeous hunk of a vampire Maxton was finally leaving the jungle.

She'd put on her favorite black lace top and skirt just for the occasion. Though she always felt her long auburn hair and sultry lips were her best features, most of her prior lovers had been into her legs. They were pretty nice, even if on the shorter side. She was a petite gal at five feet three.

I hope Maxton likes big personalities in tiny packages. She scooted closer to him on the plane about to take off, the armrest digging into her hip. "So, what do you want to see first when we get to LA?"

Maxton stared ahead like a mindless zombie, still wearing his extremely worn-out, ancient suit. The thing looked like a relic from a Jane Austen zombie film. Smelled a little musty, too.

"You still reeling over that helicopter ride?" she asked. "Trust me, you're not the only one. Brutus flies that thing like a crackhead."

Maxton stared, clearly in shock.

"You're probably wondering what a crackhead is. I can explain later. But there's nothing to be afraid of on this plane. It's like a giant metal bird that—"

"Silence." Maxton flashed a palm. "I know what an airplane is. I have watched them fly overhead for nearly a century."

"Sorry. I was just trying to—"

"I know what you are trying to do, MF." He said her name like it was a curse. "But your cordiality will not convince me to change you. I will not change anyone."

How did he know that was what she wanted?

MF's insides twisted. "Yes, I want to be a vampire again, but that's not the only reason I'm trying to be helpful." *Or get closer to you.*

"Be as helpful as you like. It will not alter my feelings."

"Because you think being a vampire is a curse?" she asked.

"I will not change you because you are...annoying, and you talk too much. Do you honestly believe I wish to be bonded to a chatty peasant of poor education and upbringing?"

MF's jaw dropped. She'd heard a lot of mean things in her twenty-five years of life, but this was in a category all its own.

She got up, went to the back of the plane, and sat next to Damien.

"Everything okay?" he asked.

"He's a fucking dick," she whispered.

"I heard that, peasant!" Maxton bellowed from the front of the plane. "Vampire hearing!"

She snarled. "I wouldn't let that monster turn me if he were the last vampire on earth."

Damien cocked a brow at her.

"You know what I mean," she said with a sigh.

"Please do not start causing problems, MF. I need the vampire's help, and he's less likely to do so if he's annoyed."

"I was just trying to be polite. He doesn't look like he's feeling so great."

Damien grumbled, "I need to get intoxicated."

She blinked at him. Damien drank, but he never had more than one or two. "Am I really that annoying?"

"Yes, but my groin hurts. I cannot figure out why."

"Okay...Good to know."

"I'm going to go up front and check on our

guest. Would you mind bringing us a bottle of whatever spirits Brutus has stowed away?" he asked.

"Sure. I'll be right up." She watched Damien go to the front of the plane and take a seat next to Maxton.

A woman in strange camo overalls passed through the aisle. Maybe she worked here. "Oh, miss? Are you part of the crew?"

The woman glared at her. "What do you want?"

Hostile much? "Just wondering where I might find some alcohol."

"In the back. Help yourself. And don't fall out of the plane on your way there." The woman disappeared into the very front of the plane, around the corner where they had a bunch of equipment in this military-slash-people transporter. *I wonder if all Uchben women are so grumpy.*

Strange. She seemed familiar somehow.

CHAPTER FOURTEEN

Damien didn't know what had changed Maxton's mind to leave the jungle, but he worried about the second part of the deal. Would Maxton agree to meet with Cimil? Until Damien had a firm answer, he wouldn't feel at ease.

"May I?" Damien pointed to the seat beside Maxton.

"As long as you do not yammer like that MF."

Damien's hackles rose. "MF is always willing to roll up her sleeves when I need her. She is loyal, and that is all that matters."

"I do not care. I am not planning on needing her. What do you wish to discuss, tailor? Make it fast. I sense I am going to enjoy this plane ride even less than the helicopter."

"Noted." Maxton had looked like he'd been about to lose his vampire cookies on the first leg of the trip. "What did my beast say to change your mind?"

Maxton stared ahead, transfixed on something. "He said that your argument made sense. This is all."

Damien's gaze flickered with doubt. It felt too easy a response. "So, that was it? He told you to come to LA, and you simply changed your mind?"

"Yes. As I said, it all made sense. I served no purpose rotting in the jungle. Now, I will serve a purpose." Maxton's voice was almost robotic.

Something is up. Almost like he was reciting lines. "Are you amenable to seeing Cimil?"

"Yes. Of course. It is why I am going there. I must make her happy so she will allow you to choose the love of your life, Willa."

Damien swallowed hard. Maxton had clearly been given the whammy. But by whom? There was no one in his party capable of such a thing, and there certainly hadn't been any brain benders in the village.

Damien nodded, unsure if he should look a gift horse in the mouth. At least he'd get to pick one woman to save. *But which one?*

No, no, I cannot think like that, he told himself. He had to find a way to save both women. But first, he wanted to find out more about this spell placed on Maxton.

"I am glad you've come around," Damien said. "So what would it take to get you to negotiate with Cimil?"

"Negotiate about what?"

"Cimil must have big plans for you, Maxton. You're the last living vampire. That means you have significant leverage. I'm asking what it would take for you to use it."

Maxton stared. "I want to return to my lair."

"That sounds fairly easy. After this is all over—"

"No. I want to return now."

"Now?" Damien wasn't following. "I thought you wanted to go to LA with us to meet Cimil."

Maxton's eyes went blank again. "Yes. LA. Cimil. Must go."

Oh boy. His head had definitely been meddled with. "And when you get there, and you are standing in front of Cimil, all I am asking is for you to demand that both women, Sky and Willa, are allowed to live. I will still choose one for my partner, but the other cannot be killed."

"You must choose Willa. Only Willa. The other must go."

What? "Why must it be Willa?" Damien asked.

"If she dies, I will explode."

"Explode?" Damien swallowed hard. This could only be one person's work. *Willa.* He looked over his shoulder. No sign of the witch, but who else would do this?

The challenge was, he couldn't turn his back on Sky. *This spell is not going to work.* Damien's only shot at saving both women was to convince Maxton to help.

"Maxton? I need you to listen to me. Someone has put a spell in your head. I will have it removed, but only if you promise to help me. Do we have a deal?"

Maxton nodded, his eyes empty.

CHAPTER FIFTEEN

The plane ride had been hard on the vampire. Especially after Damien had had Bonbon and Gorgonzolina remove the mind fuck from Maxton's head. With just a few rounds of hugs, they'd completely drained the energy in his body without risk of death since he was a vampire. Then MF had revived him with her blood.

Sadly, there had been a moment when Maxton was biting her wrist that she looked like she was going to cry. It must've been truly disappointing when he said he would not change her.

After Maxton was back to himself and past his panic attack following takeoff, Maxton explained that a woman with straight black hair had appeared near his lair and cast a sort of spell on him. She'd told him he would leave the jungle, go to LA, and meet with Cimil. He'd then overheard her tell the beast that she planned to ensure Willa was the chosen one.

So the beast and Willa conspired during my black-out. Interesting.

"You must return me to my lair," Maxton said. "I cannot be out in the wild like this."

Strange how he called being in public "the wild," but it supported Brutus's hypothesis.

"I will," Damien assured him. "After we take care of this pending business with Cimil. In the meantime, I will be your prison guard."

Maxton narrowed his eyes.

"I cannot allow you to go off on a rampage and harm whomever you like."

"You threatening me?" Maxton asked.

"Stating a fact."

"I do not require a watchman," Maxton argued.

"You get one all the same. Non-negotiable. Also non-negotiable is stopping at my shop on the way to see Cimil. You will need a new suit before being presented to her." A lie. Cimil could not care less if people came in rags, formal wear, or in a tutu, but it was a good excuse to fulfill Damien's original offer to the vampire. Also, Maxton's tattered suit was a crime against all suits. "You cannot go wearing rags, vampire."

"I will accept your offer, but I will pay for it," Maxton said.

"With what?"

"I have gold. A considerable amount. My lair is riddled with the damned stuff. I practically trip over nuggets."

Interesting. "Maxton, my only concern is ensuring you and I are aligned. I freed you from Willa's spell, and in return, you will tell Cimil that you wish both women to remain alive."

"I am a man of my word. I will tell her."

"Thank you."

Maxton seemed to be unimpressed by the modern world as the group left the private airport in LA, where they avoided Customs and Immigration, thanks to the Uchben, who had people everywhere.

On the way to the shop, Maxton barely gave notice to the cars or billboards. He didn't even bat an eyelash at all the high-rise buildings, abandoned shopping carts, and trash. But when Maxton saw the selection of fine suits, his eyes sparked up. He chose a fine gray tweed along with a black suit, which MF promptly tailored for him.

Damien had to admit, the vampire had excellent taste right down to his choice of socks, ties, and leather shoes. Wingtips, of course.

Just before seven p.m., Damien and Maxton arrived at Cimil's home, and the vampire immediately looked on edge. Maybe it was Cimil's strange decor.

"I cannot blame you. The circus theme is very disturbing," Damien said as they waited on the doorstep cluttered with junk—toaster oven, old bicycles, and erotic figurines. Maybe Cimil was preparing for a garage sale.

Cimil jerked open the door, wearing pink lederhosen with a rainbow tube top. "You accomplished the impossible, tailor. Huzzah!"

"Cimil, may I introduce—"

"I know who this tall piece of vampire is. Welcome, Maxton. I have two of my children to sip on if you're hungry. They loved being bitten." She shrugged. "They miss the vampire thing."

Damien truly loathed this mess of a goddess. From her fashion sense to her wicked meddling, she had zero redeeming qualities. The irony was that she knew it and didn't care.

"No. Thank you," Maxton replied. "I am not hungry."

"Good, then let's get started. Follow me to my office." Cimil stepped aside to let them into the foyer.

"You stay put, tailor. I won't be long." Cimil pointed to the all-hot-pink living room with a furry couch.

Damien didn't like it but fell back.

Please pull this off, Maxton. I cannot stomach losing both women.

Though his memories of Willa had faded over the decades, he still remembered seeing her for the first time as a young man. Willamina had come with her mother to his father's shop situated in a small village near Geneva, Switzerland. Damien had been instantly smitten by her silky blonde locks, rosy cheeks, and long neck. Shortly after, she was sent off to London, into society, and wouldn't return until years later. A duchess. And more beautiful than ever.

He'd known it was wrong to sleep with her, but when she asked him to be her lover during her stay, he couldn't say no. Something about the way she looked at him was irresistible. *Like candy to my heart.*

With Sky, the experience had been completely different. She was a frantic mess when they met, and though she was beautiful, it was her entire being that captivated him. Her wits, her loyalty to her family, and her very enormous lady balls. He'd never met anyone like her. She must've felt the connection, too, because she would later return to haunt him, claiming she'd anchored her soul to him. *God, how I miss her.*

Maxton had been out of his element most of his life, so this new world did not feel so different. It was like he told the tailor: The world kept on spinning in one mundane circle. It might look different on the outside with this modern makeover, but underneath it was the same old shit hole.

He and Cimil walked past several large cages filled with people dressed in bright red wigs, round red noses, and white makeup on their faces. *The goddess keeps monsters in her home?*

"Don't mind them," Cimil said. "They're here

for naughty clown Saturday."

He made a note to avoid the clown monsters in the future. They were terrifying.

He and Cimil wove through the strange house filled with even stranger objects—marble statues of the goddess, a painting depicting her and an Egyptian pharaoh riding a unicorn, and colorful drawings of vampires eating children, drawn by children.

They kept walking until they reached a set of stairs leading under the home. "This way," she said.

"What is down there?" he asked.

"My secret fun room. Only, it's not so secret. Not much fun either."

Maxton arched a brow and followed.

The room downstairs was even more frightening than the rest of the home, with brightly colored walls and crates that jostled and rumbled against one wall. An enormous fluffy structure in the shape of a castle occupied the center of the room.

Cimil sat in the castle's entrance, bouncing on her rear, her red ponytail flopping up and down. "Okay, vampire. I'm sure you know why you're here. I need your help. The world needs your help."

"You wish me to make more vampires."

"Ding, ding, ding! You get a prize! But don't pick any of the wooden boxes. Soulless bodies don't make good pets. Just stick to the gumballs." She pointed to a large clear dome filled with balls the size of quail eggs.

He had no idea what they were, but he was not about to put balls in his mouth. "No, thank you. But I am obligated to discuss terms before we continue. The tailor does not wish to choose one of his women to die. They must both live."

Cimil halted her bouncing. "Okay. Is that all?"

"And I wish to return to my lair as soon as possible."

"Okay. Anything else?"

"And I will not be turning anyone."

Cimil stared, her nostrils flaring. "What do you mean, vampire?"

"I do not wish to change anyone. I believe I should be the last vampire. Forever."

"Are you mad?"

"Vampires are dangerous. They are selfish and greedy and kill indiscriminately just for fun. The world will be a far better place without us."

"Yeah. No duh, you big duh-head. Why do you think I want them back?"

He blinked. This goddess truly lived up to her reputation. She was nonsensical. "I do not know."

"The Universe is all about balance. How can one appreciate the beauty of sunshine unless there's night? Cold days, warm days. Stinky socks, clean socks." Cimil exhaled. "I'm afraid that there just isn't enough evil in the world these days with all the immortals gone, so people are just not appreciating life like they used to. And now, because of that, humans are just getting more and more evil."

"But you just said the problem was a lack of evil."

"Lack of the right kind of evil," she said. "If we don't restore balance and start bringing back the evil creatures with very long lifespans, hell will soon fill up with all these terrible, rotten humans. We'll run out of space! And that means they'll overflow into the Underworld. Or, as I call it, the upstairs room where souls play poker until they decide if they want to have another go in a people suit or rejoin the cosmos's energy soup. But if the Underworld fills up, then there'll be no room at the tables."

How was it that the Creator decided to make this hairbrained lunatic immortal? "I am not following, goddess."

"People's souls will have nowhere to go! Then humans will stop dying. Except, they'll still die. Only they won't."

"Errr…" Maxton tilted his head to one side. "Dead but not dead? Like me?"

"No, no, Fangy-Cakes. Nothing like you. Imagine the planet filled with dead people who can't die—all rotting and diseased, not to mention stinky. Do you want the entire planet to become one enormous trash heap of undead?"

Frankly, he could not care less.

She continued, "All you need to do is give your blood to a few people on a list I've made, and all will be right in the world again. Is that so much to ask?" She pulled a folded piece of paper from her front pocket and held it up.

"I must respectfully decline."

Cimil's face turned as red as her hair. Fine by him. Maybe he would get lucky, and she would kill him.

Cimil got up and began pacing the room, speaking into thin air. "Yes. An excellent idea, Minktoid." Cimil pointed a gaunt finger at him. "What if I could offer you the one thing you've always wanted? I can make you mortal again. And in forty or so years, you'll die. No more waiting for someone stronger and fiercer to come and kill you. You'll just kaput!"

Maxton's cold heart started to rattle with glee. *An end to my suffering?* "You can do that?"

"I can't, but I know someone who can."

I could die. Finally, legitimately die. As a good Catholic. Who obviously has much killing to repent for. "May I have a few days to think it over?"

"I can give you until midnight tomorrow. Any more than that, we risk some of the people on that list croaking. Tractor deaths are on the rise."

He was unsure what a tractor was, but all right. "I will give you my reply tomorrow."

She handed him the piece of paper. "You might want to give this a read while you're chewing on my proposal."

He placed the paper in his pocket.

She added, "Oh, and you are to tell no one of my offer, vampire. I mean it. If you do, it's off."

He nodded and left the horrible room to find Damien waiting upstairs.

"Well?" Damien asked eagerly. "How did it go?"

"I am unsure."

"Did Cimil agree to let both women live?"

What part of *he was unsure* sounded confusing? "I did my part and asked. I suggest you discuss the goddess's answer with her yourself. I will wait outside. This place makes me uneasy." Too many colors.

CHAPTER SIXTEEN

Damien was officially in panic mode. Cimil had refused to change her mind. Why was she so set on inflicting suffering?

And then she has the gall to offer up advice as if she were my friend? Her exact words were, "I suggest instead of thinking with your long hard one, you think long and hard about what you're getting on the inside. You have until the end of the day tomorrow to make your choice. Sky, the woman who lights up your heart? Or Willa, the woman who broke it?"

For fuck's sake. If it came down to his heart, of course he'd choose Sky. She was a good woman who always wanted to do right. She inspired him to be a better man. No, that was wrong. Also, a cliché.

She inspires me to be less of a deadly selfish bastard.

Willa was the opposite, though that didn't negate the fact he still felt deeply for her. They had history. Long ago, he loved her. She once carried his child. How could he let her die?

Damien entered his house, which he'd obtained

as payment during his time as a fixer. One of his clients, a vampire before the Great Explosion, had been filmed drinking five women. It had taken several weeks and thousands in bribes to clean up the mess, and this house had been given as payment. Five bedrooms, infinity pool, outdoor bar, rooftop lounging area, spacious garage, and a five-hundred-square-foot closet just for his suits. All overlooking Sunset.

"I'm ready for a night of greasy chow mein, fine scotch, and a hot shower," Damien grumbled, placing his delivery order on the app as they entered the living room. He'd barely had time to clean up or eat after arriving home this afternoon. "Maxton, there is a basement that belonged to the prior owner—his vampire sex dungeon. It's now a wine cellar, but…" Damien looked up to see the entire gang assembled. "What the hell are you all doing here?"

"I thought you might want company," said Bonbon, sitting on Damien's white sofa next to Gorgonzolina and Pet with a giant bowl of popcorn. A movie with talking dogs played on the TV.

Not again. The last time they'd had movie night, they left grease stains and fur all over the fabric. Took him three days to clean it.

Damien exhaled slowly with contempt. "I just spent…an entire week…in the jungle…with you imbeciles. And I *distinctly* recall dropping you all off at the shop earlier and telling you to make yourselves scarce." He needed to rest. "Leave."

"Okay, we'll stay and keep you and Maxton company." Pet looked at Maxton. "I can help you shower if you like. I'm very handy with a loofa. Also, handies." She winked.

Damien winced. "I do not advise letting her anywhere near your genitals, Maxton. She has very sharp teeth."

Maxton gave Damien a look.

"I did not mean she has bitten my penis during a sex act. I am not into fairies or their kink. I merely meant she is not to be trusted."

"You are a mean man, Damien Greystone. Oh look! Your favorite scotch." She flew straight for the bottle and began gyrating on the neck.

"There, you see," said Damien to Maxton. "She has sworn a thousand times to stop molesting my liquor."

"This is all very interesting," Maxton said drably, "but I think I will take up your offer of the downstairs wine cave."

"But I thought, maybe, we could go out?" MF interjected, appearing in the doorway wearing tight jeans, suede Victorian boots, and a shiny pleather corset. Lots of cleavage. Her long auburn hair was curled, flowing over her shoulders. "We can hit the mall—it's open for another hour, and there are five different suit stores there."

"Did you say suits?" Maxton arched a dark brow, his eyes flickering down at MF's goods.

Damien didn't care if he was or wasn't into MF, but there was one problem. "I cannot—"

"And after that," MF said to Maxton, "we can try the roller coaster at the amusement park. It's best at night. Much scarier."

"I'm not afraid of a...what did you call it?" Maxton asked.

"But I—" Damien attempted to interject but was cut off again.

"A roller coaster," MF said. "And you don't even know what that is, so how can you say you're not scared?"

"Anything called by that name will never frighten me."

"I'm sorry to nip this in the bud," Damien barked, "but I'm tired, hungry, and I have some sort of rash on my cock. Feels like a friction burn. Must've been the heat. So there will be no going out, since I'm the only one who can guard Maxton."

"I do not need a nursemaid, tailor," Maxton snarled. "I am a vampire, and I will decide where I go and when." Maxton marched out the front door.

MF looked at Damien and shrugged. "I guess we're going out."

"MF, don't let his fine suit and good looks fool you. He can be extremely dangerous if he loses control. Take Bonbon and Gorgonzolina in the demon stroller with you. They can slow him down if he starts looking agitated." He turned for his room to shower. "Call me if anything comes up. Or better yet, don't." Maxton wasn't his problem anymore. The deal with Cimil was complete, and now he had to do the unthinkable: decide between Sky and Willa. His heart and guilt versus his loyalty and guilt.

"What do you think?" MF asked as she and Maxton strolled through the mall, where children on sugar highs ran with ice cream ahead of parents escaping the summer heat before bedtime. She was eager to get Maxton's reaction to this new way of shopping. *Just wait until he finds out about the internet. He'll flatline. Again.*

"I am unsure," Maxton said, frowning.

Maxton still seemed troubled after his visit with Cimil. Lots of grunting and growling under his breath. Not so dissimilar from Damien when he was struggling with something.

"You'll like this next store," she said. "It's the perfect place to take your mind off—"

A little girl in a unicorn shirt ran up, wanting to pet the Chihuahuas in her stroller. Thankfully the netting was completely closed.

"No touching," MF said sternly. "They are demons who'll suck the life force from you. Also, that shirt is evil. Now go away."

The little girl ran to the shelter of her mother's hand three stores down.

MF smiled. "Now, where was I? Ah, yes. The mall is a place people hang out for free AC—that's air cooling. It's a necessity in this part of the country."

"Cool air is for the weak," he grumbled.

"Spoken like a true—" she lowered her voice "—vampire. But for us humans, well, I'm sure you remember feeling hot in the summer." Vampires could feel heat, of course, but they were usually more worried about sunlight, which drained their energy. Left outside long enough, it could kill them.

"I was far too busy being a vampire slave to be concerned with such things."

"Vampire slave?" she whispered.

"Yes."

This was news. "But how? When?"

"My human parents sold me to my master when I was very young. He wanted me for luring unsuspecting merchants or women looking for work in his home. I would pretend to be his houseboy and greet them. Sometimes I would entertain them while I waited for my master to wake."

"Entertain?"

"Sing, juggle, recite poems he had me learn. As I grew bigger, he hired a caregiver—whom he eventually drank—to teach me to read. Then he hired a personal chef to teach me to cook, whom he drank. Then he hired a piano teacher, tailor, and gardener. Drank them all. I was the most educated, well-dressed child in all the world. And then one day, he drank me."

MF winced. What a sad, sad story. "What happened to him?"

"After he turned me? I killed him."

MF blinked. "Jesus. That sounds rough."

"He had it coming. Though, if I had been smarter, I would have waited. I'd been taught everything except for how to be a vampire. He held that back, believing it would prevent the exact scenario that ended him."

"He thought if you needed him, you'd never turn against him," MF concluded.

"Exactly."

"Fucking asshole."

"Indeed. I often wondered if he spared me as an act of cruelty."

"How so?" MF asked.

"He brought those people into his home to care for me. The moment I cared back, he took them away, and each time he allowed me to live, my guilt grew. I think he enjoyed it." Maxton smiled. "The day I killed him was the greatest joy I'd ever known, though that too came with a price; no one to guide me in the ways of the vampire."

MF was beginning to put the puzzle pieces together. Maxton had spent his entire human life hating his vampire master. Then he was left to his own devices as a new vampire and never learned control, so he ended up hating himself just as much.

"If it's any consolation," she said, "not all makers are like that, from what I've heard. Some are kind. Some are compassionate and wise."

"But most are bloodthirsty monsters. At the end of the day, vampires are what they are: evil."

"I wasn't evil. I mean, yeah, it was rough that first week after I was abandoned, but I think," she whispered the next part, "when I killed recklessly, it was more about acting out. I'd just lost my entire family. But after a few weeks, I realized that being angry and violent wasn't going to bring back my parents. It certainly wasn't honoring their memory."

"And you believe that becoming a murdering abomination again will honor them?"

"I don't think you have to be an abomination if you're a vampire. It's a choice. Just like being a good or bad human. Or demon. Just look at Gorg and Bon. Have you ever seen more loving creatures? All they want to do is cuddle and be happy. They don't let their species or origin of hellfire dictate who they are. And even if they are occasionally murderous, who's to say that killing is entirely wrong? Even the Bible believes in justice. Eye for an eye?"

He narrowed his eyes; he wasn't buying it.

"Okay. I see it like this: God made tigers, scorpions, rattlesnakes, crocodiles, and giant creepy spiders. Their jobs are to kill and maintain balance in nature. So why can't I believe that your kind wasn't made for the same reason? You have a part to play, and it's not evil unless you make it that way."

"This is all fine and good, except for one flaw in

your argument, MF. If being a giant creepy spider makes you feel miserable because you are giant and creepy, and those qualities fly in the face of everything you hold sacred, then it becomes an act of suffering. Of pain. Of relentless damnation, and there isn't a *damned* thing you can do to change it."

Whoa. I think I hit a nerve. "I thought you said you hated being a vampire because you were bored?"

"And I was truthful."

Really? Because his anger didn't sound like boredom. It sounded like a man haunted by his past. He had her deepest sympathy.

MF stared at this beautiful man, looking like a dream in his new suit as they strolled. She wanted to ease his torment. Mostly because she'd been alone during her darkest moments and wished it on no one.

"I get the feeling you're not telling the entire truth," MF said. "Totally your prerogative. But if you want to talk to someone, I promise I won't judge. I'm *so* not about that." She might dress tough—leather, spikes, torn jeans, tits out half the time—but that was only to shield the gooey center.

"Do *you* tell everything to perfect strangers?" he asked.

"No, but I'd tell you. Anything you want."

He stopped walking, and so did she.

"Why?" he asked.

"Because I like you. And before you claim I just want you to—" she looked over her shoulder at a group of teens nearby, lowering her voice "—to turn me, that's not it at all."

"You like me?" He chuckled snidely.

"Insult my integrity if you want, but as far as I'm concerned, you have no reason to doubt me. I haven't said or done anything to make you believe I'm not one hundred percent transparent. I am as good-hearted as they come."

"Yet you want to change into a violent, blood-thirsty creature."

She pointed to her heart. "Won't change this. Nothing ever has."

Maxton stared for a long moment, his green eyes smoldering. "Show me this nirvana of gentle-men's wear you speak of."

She smiled. "My pleasure."

CHAPTER SEVENTEEN

MF couldn't believe how different Maxton was acting suddenly, as if the whole ritual of wearing gentlemen's clothing relaxed him. Maybe because it was something familiar and comforting, like sewing. For her, sewing wasn't "women's work" or "antiquated," as some of the younger, more "progressive" generation claimed. Sewing was an art where imagination met engineering. The engineering of fabrics.

She wasn't just talking about fashion designers. She was talking about the everyday seamstress, the tailor, the home sewer, the quilter and embroiderer. One might even argue that crocheting was engineering.

One could have all the ideas in the world—skirts that flowed like waterfalls, dresses that shimmered and moved with the light, dress shirts that gave a man an air of sophistication, or even a simple pillowcase for Aunt Fanny—but that idea meant nothing without execution. Perfect angles. Perfect cuts on the bias. Perfect fabric selection and stitching. Precision. That was what she loved about the art.

She was partial to complicated vampires, too.

MF, Maxton, and the two napping demons in the doggy stroller exited the men's clothing store with over ten thousand dollars' worth of suits for Maxton, and he looked happier than a clam in wet sand.

The funny part was when he went to pay, Maxton simply waved his hand and said: "IOU. The gold will be in the post by week's end. I must return home first."

The salesperson just nodded and wrapped it all up.

"So, what do you say we head to the amusement park next?" MF asked. "I think we have about two hours before they close."

They stepped out into the cool summer air. He inhaled and exhaled with a cough. "This air smells funny."

"Yeah. LA. Whatcha gonna do?"

"I would like to see this coaster of rolls. Take me there," he said.

MF smiled. It was such a glorious thing to see this man shedding that big chip on his shoulder.

Suddenly, he turned, staring down at her. "But I am hungry."

"So soon?" MF blinked.

"My diet has been very limited these past years, and we have been very active today—all that helicoptering and aeroplaning."

"Ah. That." MF nodded. "I can see if—"

"You. I want you now. We shall go to your automobile." He walked off toward her new black Range Rover. She'd just bought it last week since her old car died.

MF's heart skipped a beat. He wanted to drink from her again?

She inhaled slowly and exhaled. On the plane, it had made her come so hard that she saw stars. Of course, she had to hide it and act like she was in pain. Damien had looked at her with so much pity.

MF followed him. "Maxton, I…"

"Yes?" He raised a dark brow, standing by the passenger-side door.

She wanted to be transparent, but this was kind of embarrassing.

"Hurry now," Maxton urged. "I do not want to lose control."

She nodded tightly and pressed the key fob. "You can put the bags in the back."

Maxton stored the clothes, and they got in the SUV. She started the engine and cranked up the AC.

"Jus-just give me a minute." She flipped on the radio and turned up the volume. Maybe it would drown out her moans.

She glanced at Maxton, whose hungry green eyes were locked on her neck.

She swallowed hard. He wasn't interested in her

wrist this time. "Um, can you make it fast? I don't want to get to the park too late." But really, she didn't want him making her orgasm again.

"I'll make it very fast." He leaned toward her, and she moved her long hair out of the way, exposing her neck. He inhaled deeply. "You smell very exotic."

"Exotic?" she asked.

"Human, but with notes of bitterness."

"Oh. I'm sorry."

"Do not be," he said. "I like it. Reminds me of the ale I used to drink as a child."

"Beer for kids. How 1700s." She chuckled nervously.

"Do not be afraid." He rubbed his hand over her shoulder.

"It's just that I usually did the neck nibbling. Not the other way around."

"I am quite skilled at this," he said. "No pain. I promise."

"Okay." She leaned closer, and he bent his head, burying her face in his long silky hair. He smelled incredible—like freshly cut cedar on a spring morning.

She inhaled deeply and then—*chomp!*

"Ow!" she yelled, feeling his fangs puncture the sensitive skin.

He wrapped his arms around her to stop her from wiggling and began drawing on the wound.

The pain quickly turned into something very

pleasurable.

"Oh boy. That-that's nice." First, it felt like a tickle in her neck, but as his mouth sucked and massaged, the tickle moved down, down, down.

"Oh, wow." She grabbed onto his arm. "That is...wow...wow..." The tickle escalated into a sensual throb, radiating from her core, outward through her entire body. Even down there. *Oh crap. That's fantastic.* It felt like being fucked from the inside. "Don't stop. Don't stop." *Yes, yes, I needed this. He's amazing.*

The throbbing turned to an erotic pounding, hitting her between the legs. She was about to come.

"Mmmm..." he moaned.

The deep timber of his voice pushed her to the edge of the cliff. More throbbing and pounding. "Oh God. Oh God. I'm going to—"

Maxton unlatched his mouth and licked his lips. "Thank you. That was very nourishing."

MF blinked, her heart racing. "Oh, no you don't, vampire. You finish me off."

"You wish me to kill you?" He frowned, confused.

"Not that kind of finish. The other kind. You know—that thing you were just doing that made me feel like—"

"If I bring you to climax, your heart will stop."

"Not true. I had my special moment on the plane."

He cocked his head to one side. "You did?"

"It brought tears to my eyes." She felt embarrassed telling him, but it was more important to get him to continue.

"Are you certain?"

"Yes, Maxton! I'm young, but not naïve." *Finish me!*

"You climaxed and did not die. How unusual." He looked out the window to his side, pondering.

"Hey. Can we just postpone the thinking? I'm kinda spinning right now." She exposed her neck again.

"But I—"

"Do it, or I'll stake you when you sleep tonight," she growled.

He smiled but didn't go in for another bite. "I just realized something about you."

That I'm horny, and it's your fault?

He brushed a lock of hair from her face. "Your parents could not have bestowed a more fitting name upon you, Mountain Flower."

"Pfft! I'm anything but delicate or pretty. My parents were just hippies who loved nature." *Now O me, dude. Seriously!*

He stared with those intense eyes. "That is not what your name means. They understood, as I now do, that your two biggest traits are your unmovable strength—like a mountain. Yet you are not afraid to feel or care. You have a kind, delicate nature. Like a flower."

MF's mouth slacked as his words sank in. Her

parents always said they picked her name because it represented what they wanted her to be. She always thought they wanted her to be pretty and naturally feminine.

Frankly, it never made sense because that wasn't her at all and made her feel like she wasn't living up to their expectations. While she loved being a woman, she wasn't demure or quiet or overtly prissy. She was more like a cactus, if you asked her. A little prickly, but pretty in its own way. But now, after all these years, this vampire had figured out what they'd really meant.

"I can't believe I never saw it." Tears formed in her eyes. "Thank you."

"For?"

"For healing an old wound." She pressed her hand over her heart. "They did see me."

"As do I."

MF's heart began beating faster. She knew he could hear it. "Are you still game for that coaster of rolls?"

Maxton flashed a warm smile. "Indeed."

CHAPTER EIGHTEEN

When MF parked her black Range Rover, she was still suffering from residual flutters. They had an hour before the park closed, plenty of time to do a few rides, but her stomach was a mess.

She hugged her midriff, unsure if the waves inside weren't being caused by her supertight corset, that moment back at the mall, or all the clicking in her head.

From the first moment she'd laid her eyes on Maxton in the jungle, the wanting began. The gnawing, the carnal ache. He had been unconscious, covered in mud, wearing only a white dress shirt. From the looks of his bloody, bruised body, one might think he was in pain, but the big smile on his lips told a different story.

That was the moment she just knew. He wasn't some ordinary vampire. This guy was fun! He loved a fair fight. He enjoyed being what he was. She wanted that kind of vampire by her side.

To her surprise, though, after Maxton was awake, he told a completely different tale. One she didn't buy. Somewhere, beneath the layers of jungle sweat and dirt, was a great man just waiting to be happy.

I can help with that! she'd thought.

And now, after he'd said the thing about her name, all she could hear was *click, click, click*!

Click, he sees me for who I really am.

Click, the more I get to know him, the more connected I feel.

Click, he gave me a "cookie" without killing me.

MF felt simultaneously terrified and giddy. Could Maxton be her special someone?

She'd heard random comments from the few immortals she hung out with about this thing called "a mate," like with Bonbon and Gorgonzolina. They believed there was only one person handpicked by the Universe to be your special someone. That didn't mean a person couldn't love another, but they would never be a perfect match.

MF sighed as she watched a couple stroll past holding hands. Could that be her and Maxton in the future?

"Are you having difficulties breathing?" Maxton asked.

"Oh. No. I'm just a little tired. That's all. Maybe I donated too much blood today." She winked.

"I am not a big eater, so that cannot be the cause."

Time to divert his attention.

MF pointed to the ride she was itching to go on.

"Look. There it is! The Wiggly Tornado of Death! It's rated the scariest ride in North America."

Maxton stopped walking, his eyes moving up, down, and side to side. He had excellent vision, especially at night, so he was likely checking out the sick turns.

"Well?" MF said. "You want to try?"

Maxton scoffed. "This is nothing compared to how I move."

Oh boy. That sounded very sexy. Her cheeks grew hot as she imagined him naked, pumping himself between her thighs.

"Are you nervous?" Maxton asked. "Your face is flushed."

God, what this vampire does to me. "I'm good." She took his hand. "Come on! Let's hurry. The line's not too long, so we should be able to go a few times."

⌒ ⌒

MF had never seen a vampire vomit, and for the record, it wasn't pretty—all that blood shooting from his mouth onto a grassy patch outside the ride.

Thankfully, it's nighttime.

A family strolled by, their eyes filling with terror as the light from the Ferris wheel to their side caught the red of Maxton's vomit.

MF chuckled awkwardly. "Too much cherry slushy."

The family scurried off.

Maxton stood upright, inhaling through his nostrils with his eyes closed.

"Maxton? Are you all right? Can I get you anything? I don't know what to do. I've never seen this happ—"

Maxton doubled over again, launching red meaty chunks from his mouth.

"Oh, wow." MF looked away. "Was that your entire stomach that just came out? I'm so sorry. I had no idea you'd get this—"

"Grrr…" Maxton stood, his eyes black and a snarl on his bloody mouth.

Was he about to turn into unstoppable killer Maxton? *Oh, shit.* The demons were asleep in the car.

"Maxton," MF held out her hands, "you're going to have to calm down. Let's just get you to the car, okay? Then I can give you a refill, and you'll feel much better."

"Grrr…" His eyes whipped to the arcade a few yards away, opposite them. It was fairly busy.

And he looks hangry.

He zipped away from her.

Where'd he go? She turned her head to find his silhouette in the arcade's doorway.

"Maxton! No!" She bolted, her arms pumping and legs moving far too slowly to compete with a vampire's speed. "Stay right there!" She was almost to him just as he disappeared inside.

"Shit! Shit! *Shit!*" She needed Damien, but by the time he got here, the entire park would be dead.

MF rushed past a group of teens trying to win a prize from the claw machine. She hung a right down another row of retro arcade games, glancing at *Pac-Man*. At this moment, that was probably Maxton, mowing down rows of unsuspecting humans. Chomp, chomp, chomp!

"Maxton! Whatever the fuck you're doing right now, you'd better…" MF turned the next corner by the air hockey and froze. Maxton was standing there holding up some kid by the neck with his left hand while looking at another kid in his right hand.

"Fuck!" MF charged, tackling Maxton and sacking his ass to the ground. He must've not seen her coming because he probably outweighed her by fifty or sixty pounds.

Maxton hit the concrete floor with a *thump!* He released the two children, who immediately began screaming bloody murder.

Good choice. Run, you little boogers! Run!

Now on top of Maxton, MF knew she only had a fraction of a second to get through to him.

"Snap out of it!" MF raised her arm and back-handed him across the cheek. "Ow!" That hurt. His face was solid granite. *Think, MF! Think!*

She stared at his lips, transfixed by their glossy sheen. She leaned over and pressed her mouth to his.

He didn't move—a very good thing. MF kept

her mouth to his for a moment more, unable to resist twisting her neck to the side a little. His lips were surprisingly soft. She'd give him some tongue, but in his state, he might bite it off. Instead, she broke away and pushed her neck to his mouth.

Before she could take one breath, he latched on, cupping the back of her head.

"Eww! They're making out," said someone in the background.

MF didn't care who was watching or that they only had a few seconds to blow this pop stand before security showed up.

Maxton's mouth worked over the bite, sucking and massaging.

Oh God. That feels so good. She pressed her hands to the floor on either side of his head and relaxed into it.

First came the tickle, then the throbbing, and then…pounding. *Boom!*

"Yes. Yes!" she cried out, feeling the valley between her legs pulse with erotic waves as she straddled him. It was better than any sex she'd ever had, though if Maxton offered to bed her right here and now, she'd take it. He was incredible with that mouth.

Imagine what the rest of him is capable of!

Maxton broke away from her neck, licking his lips.

She turned her head to face him and found stunning green eyes, alert and sharply focused on her mouth.

"You stopped my rampage," he said, dumb-founded.

"I sure did." She was just as shocked as he was. "But now we need to skedaddle."

She climbed off him, and Maxton quickly got to his feet.

"Allow me to make our exit hastier." He held out his hand.

She stared at it for a quick second. This was the same vampire who'd given her a death threat just a few days ago. *And now he's offering his hand?* She didn't have to force him or sneak it in like earlier when she'd dragged him onto that ride.

She slid her hand into his, and he swiftly whipped her around, gripping her in his iron embrace by the waist. "Close your eyes."

"No way." She wanted to see every blurry second of traveling at vampire speed again.

CHAPTER NINETEEN

Damien woke the next morning with a splitting headache. Likely a beast hangover with a side of jetlag. *Or a side of nightmare.* That whole episode in the jungle felt like a never-ending bad dream, but thankfully it was over.

Damien sat up slowly, the fog in his mind moving out to sea.

"Crap. Not over." Tonight he had to tell Cimil which woman he chose, but here was the thing: Yesterday, he would've chosen Sky. But today, with a fresh mind, he realized that Willa was the only reason he was getting a choice at all.

Underhanded or not, her witchery had gotten Maxton to leave the jungle.

Damien ran a hand through his hair, which was almost due for a cut. Or maybe he'd let it grow out again. Maxton had a splendid head of longish dark hair. *Goes well with a black suit.*

Damien climbed out of bed and made his way to his lavish marble bathroom for his morning ritual—a brief stay in the sauna to sweat out the scotch and whatever junk food he'd had for dinner, followed by an exfoliation session.

In the old days, he never cared for himself this way. They had soap made of fat and lye. He bathed once a week if weather and wood stores permitted. He certainly never owned cologne or manly scented moisturizers that reminded him of long walks in the forest on an autumn morn.

But as he'd grown older and more isolated from the world, he began seeking out what modern humans called "the little things." All the small comforts that helped one pass the day and forget about the woes of life.

Damien dabbed on some aftershave, even though he hadn't shaved. *Why bother?* He wasn't in the mood to put on airs today. Choosing Willa meant denying his primal urge to couple with Sky and to make a cozy, comfortable life filled with travel, lovemaking, and long breakfasts by the seaside at the tropical island villa he would buy for her. Of course, he'd have to find plenty of diversions for Sky, because a woman like her did not sit still for long. *I wonder if she enjoys decoupage.*

There was a loud pounding on his bedroom door.

"Damien! You in there?"

"Sky?" His heart hopscotched through his stomach, giddy to see her again. "One moment. I am dressing!"

He went to his closet to grab a white undershirt

and slacks but then paused. He reached for his bathrobe instead. Maybe she was here for what he wanted her to be here for. Yes, yes. Sex. With corporeal bodies. Not that the ghost sex hadn't been interesting.

He went for the door and opened it, finding that same, earth-shattering attraction pulsating under his skin for her. Didn't matter that physically Sky was now blonde instead of brunette or that her face was completely different. It hadn't been her beauty that had originally caught his eye. It was her spirit.

"Hello, Damien." Sky blinked her big green eyes at him. She wore her hair up in a ponytail and had on tight jeans and a snug blue blouse. He could make out every curve of her feminine body—small pert breasts, lean legs, narrow waist.

I can work with that. His groin began to stir.

"Where the hell have you been?" he barked, immediately regretting his tone. Desperation had come out like a reprimand.

"Trying to put my life back together after some-one ran me over with his SUV."

"You know how deeply sorry I feel about that. I merely meant that I have been worried for you." He drew a long breath. "Are you all right?"

"No. And yes. But that's why I'm here."

Her serious tone set off warning bells. "All right."

"Damien," she drew a quick breath, "I think I

was given this opportunity to live again because I have unfinished business."

He cocked his head, attempting to decipher. Cimil had brought her back to be at his side. "What business?"

"I died before I could tell the world what SBP was up to. Today, I changed that."

Damien's heart leapt from his stomach and onto the floor. Facedown. Pounding its fists. "What did you do, Sky?" he growled.

"I published the final article with the receipts. It included every document, piece of video, the human victims' testimonies, cell phone records, and even geo-location tracking that lines up with every claim in the report."

"You-you told the world that there is a secret organization trafficking humans and supernatural creatures for the sole purpose of growing immortal bodies?"

Sky nodded.

Damien unleashed a laugh so loud that it rattled his own eardrums.

"What the hell's so funny?" Sky scowled.

"No one will believe you."

"I can name twenty things off the top of my head that no one would've believed ten or twenty years ago. Make it a million things if you go back one thousand years. But eventually, Damien, the truth comes out. Earth isn't flat. Men aren't gods— even if I could be persuaded to worship the right one—and women shouldn't be shoved into mud huts during their moon cycles. The world evolves. And when this world becomes enlightened enough to accept that humans aren't at the top of the food chain, and there is more than one realm, they'll look back at my article and know that I was telling the truth. Except, I put your name on it."

"My name is on the article?"

She nodded, her mouth twisting to one side.

"Why the hell would you do that? You are putting me, MF, Pet, Gorgonzolina, and Bonbon at risk."

"But you said no one will believe me," she snapped back.

Damien rubbed his brow. He did not need another mess right now.

He gestured toward the sitting area by the window, overlooking the city below. "Please."

Sky went over and took a seat. He sat across from her, taking a moment to cool down. He did not want to lose his patience with her or fight. Not when he missed her so much.

Damien muted his temper. "Sky, no one will believe you except the people who know it's the truth. And they won't be pleased you're going public—especially the part about trafficking women." The governor's deceased brother had founded SBP, but from what Damien could tell, their circle of powerful friends and the governor himself were all in on it. These were not nice people.

"Good, because I started this entire thing to save them. Whether they're taken and used for sex or ultimately end up in an SBP lab to have their souls sucked from their bodies against their will and implanted into one of these," she pointed to herself, "it's vile and needs to stop."

"I agree, Sky." In fact, he admired her determination to get the truth out there. It was the reason he'd felt instantly attracted when they met. "But what I do not understand is why you published under my name."

"I knew you wouldn't be happy about it, but the world thinks I'm dead, and I couldn't have Governor Newbery and his buddies thinking it was my sister Amelia's doing. They'd immediately suspect her if I didn't put your name on it."

"Then why not use an alias?" he asked.

"Because for anyone to believe a word of it, the report had to come from a real person. And who better than a deadly, immortal tailor who was once an assassin and now works for a dangerous goddess."

"If I had to choose between Amelia or myself as a target, I would make the same decision; however, if I were truly after justice, I would rely on this." He tapped the side of his head. "I have destroyed far more villains by outsmarting them than I ever did with a sword."

"You used a sword to kill people?"

"It's quiet. Doesn't draw attention." He

shrugged. "And if you want to take down SBP, you must do the same. You must become one of them, Sky. You must work for the people at the top."

"What?"

"You died," he said. "Now you have a new body, a new face, and, with my help, a new identity, too. We can cater your résumé and background to appeal to the governor himself. And after you have earned his trust, you can collect all the information you need to take him down. Quietly. Discreetly. For good.'"

Her green eyes flickered with mischief. "What if I don't want quiet? What if I want him to have to face the world for exploiting those poor women?"

"Then you search for evidence to do just that. However, I recommend finding something you can show to his enemies."

"I don't follow," she said.

"Men like him always have enemies—other wealthy, powerful people. Find something that will provoke his enemies to take him out."

Sky nodded. "I see; let his enemies do the dirty work."

"Exactly." This was one of the key strategies he once used as a fixer. Avoid taking down powerful people head-on. Never ended well. But find out who their biggest enemies were, and then fuel those people to act? Very effective.

"Okay," she said. "But what if that doesn't stop him and his cronies? What if in the meantime, the trafficking continues? How about the poor super-natural critters who get swept up in their nets? Cimil might've burned down SBP's headquarters, but we both know that can't be their only operation."

"You must weigh the end goal with the cost of getting there. How many innocent lives will be lost for the sake of ending SBP for good? It is a decision you must make because the burden will be yours to bear." He reached over and took her hand. "Just know that I am here for you. Even if I am incredibly annoyed that you used me as a nom de plume."

A demure smile flashed across her lips, and the two stared at each other for a long moment. Her gaze floated down to his mouth, a subtle invitation to kiss her perhaps.

He was about to go in when he remembered something important. *Fuck.*

"Sky, I need to tell you something."

"Sounds ominous." She leaned back, reclaiming her hand.

"Cimil has backed me into a corner. She is demanding that I choose between you and Willa."

Sky rolled her eyes. "I can already guess how that's going to shake out."

"Why do you say that?"

She shot him a look. "Willa was your first love."

"If only it were so simple."

She raised a gold eyebrow. "So you're not choosing her?"

"I did not say that. What I meant is that—"

"Never mind. I gotta go, Damien. Have a nice life." She stood to leave.

"Sky, wait." He stood and grabbed her arm. "I want to choose you. I do."

"Well, I don't want you to. Because if you did pick me, you'll always be feeling guilty that you turned your back on Willa." She threw her hands in the air. "Cimil's made it so no matter what you do, I can't win. And neither can you. Not unless I make the choice for you, which I just did."

"But, Sky, you don't under—"

"Damien, I'll be fine. Hearts heal. And look at all the stuff I have to be grateful for. A second chance at life. I can hug my sister and nephew again. I might even get to live forever in this body."

Damien's heart sank to the abyss of his soul. "No. You won't, Sky. That's the catch. Cimil will execute the woman I do not select. I have until the end of the day."

CHAPTER TWENTY

Willa couldn't believe how wonderful this new modern world was! People were dumber than ever and so easy to control.

For example, take this room the hotel staff called "the penthouse" with a big bed, modern gadgets, and fine upholstered furniture in autumn tones, all overlooking a glorious park! All for free! And they even brought food to her room on a small rolling table.

"I'm so glad that taxi man brought me here." She crunched down on a thing called an egg roll. "Where's the egg?" She shrugged and kept chewing.

After she finished eating and figuring out how to use the bathing chamber with magnificent indoor plumbing, she would throw on one of the new outfits she'd obtained from the small store in the hotel's greeting area. *Also free!*

Then she would make the man downstairs summon a ride to take her to see Damien. She had not had the chance to ensure Damien chose her today—not that she had anything to worry about—

but why risk it?

Maybe I can get that beast to come out and play again. And she knew just the mind trick to make it happen. *I can't wait.* She had never experienced such savage pleasure as she had with the beast in that jungle. He took her like an insatiable madman, leaving her deliciously sore and limp. Damien had never made her feel like that.

Maybe after Damien chose her, which he would, she might remove him from the equation altogether. *Put the beast completely in control forever.*

The beast would make the perfect weapon and, of course, lover.

A loud buzz echoed through the suite.

What is that?

Buzzz!

There it was again. "Hello? Is someone there?" She looked up and around. "Reveal yourself."

"Willa! It's Cimil!" a voice called from outside the room.

Cimil's here? This could not be good. Nothing involving the goddess ever was.

Willa got up, closed her pink silk robe, and opened the door. Cimil stood there in a sparkly shirt and white pants that shone like glass.

Odd clothing, but what did Willa know? She'd been dead for almost two hundred years.

"Cimil, do come in. I am sorry to say these accommodations do not come with a butler or servants of any kind, but there is a magic box on that table. If you press six, a woman will answer and make suggestions of strange foods to eat, which then appear at the door in about twenty minutes." Willa looked at the dining table, where her food was laid out. "At the moment I am eating something called an egg roll, but I think they forgot the eggs. Would you care for one?"

"No, thank you, sugar. I'm still digesting the roasted pig I ate yesterday." Cimil walked over to the sitting area and plopped down on the stuffed purple chair. "I'm gonna make this quick, Willa." Cimil pointed to the armchair across from her. "Sit."

Willa did not like the sound in Cimil's voice, but she sat anyway. What choice did she have?

"I'll cut to the chase," Cimil said. "I know what you did."

Willa winced. *Oh no. How did she find out?* "I understand why you are upset, Cimil; however, I had every right to follow Damien to the jungle. After all, you told me I had to be his partner, so that is what I did. I partnered. Without him seeing me."

"Not talking about that, Queen of Mean. I'm talking about you giving the whammy to my vampire. Did you honestly think you would get away with it?"

Oh. That. "I can explain. I overheard Damien speaking about the ultimatum you gave him along with the requirement to get Maxton to LA. So I just decided to ensure his success."

"By telling Maxton to explode himself if you weren't chosen and died? Tsk-tsk." Cimil clicked her tongue.

"I wanted insurance. You of all beings know how treacherous you can be."

"True and true. But what displeases me is that Maxton came all this way and refuses to do my evil bidding. This will not stand." Cimil made a fist and slammed it down on the coffee table.

"Well, I got him to LA," Willa said. "I'm sure I can get him to do whatever else you like. Just as soon as Damien announces he has chosen me—"

"Oh, no, pumpkin. That is where you're mistaken. Your brainwashing failed. Damien removed all your handiwork before Maxton even landed in LA."

How the hell did he remove her spell?

Cimil continued, "I think you overestimate the hold you have over others, including Damien. In fact, if I were to place a bet, I'd say he's going to choose Sky tonight."

No. Not possible. "Well, well, I'm sure you're wrong. He and I go way back. He loves me and always has."

"Ah, but what if someone were to tell him that he never really loved you because you put a spell on him? What would he say then?" Cimil flashed a wicked smile.

Willa started to fume. Who did this goddess think she was? "Damien would have fallen for me anyway. I merely tinkered with the timeline."

"Bwap!" Cimil made an X with her arms. "Wrong answer. But here is what I'm willing to do. I won't tell Damien the truth, and in exchange, you'll do a favor for me."

"What do you want?" Willa narrowed her eyes.

"I want you to turn Maxton into a mortal—remove his vampirism."

"You—you want to make him mortal? Why?"

"That is my bologna to roll. Yes or no, Willa?" Cimil pushed.

Willa wasn't certain she could make him human again. Generally, syphoning off someone's supernatural energy and powers involved transferring them to someone else. *Guess I'll have to make it work.* "So you promise to let Damien choose me then?"

"I promise not to tell Damien that he never loved you and it was all an illusion. But he still gets to choose on his own. Deal?"

Willa's mind tripped on something. Why would Cimil want to change Maxton after all that trouble getting him here to LA? It wasn't adding up.

A light bulb went off.

Cimil just said a few moments ago that Maxton didn't want to do Cimil's evil bidding. *Unless he can be persuaded! Maxton wants to be human again.*

Willa smiled. "I'll turn your vampire back to human, but what I want in return is something else. I want the beast." Willa raised her chin. "Get rid of

Damien."

Cimil stared in shock. "You are one backstabbing viper. I like it! But no can do. I need Damien."

"Why? So he can do your dirty work? I'll be a thousand times better at it. Especially with the beast by my side. He's merciless."

"But if you're wrong, I'm stuck without my sheriff." Cimil scratched her chin. "How about this? I can give the beast an SBP body, and you can have a trial. If you make me happy, we'll talk."

"There are more bodies?" Willa had heard that the lab responsible for making her and Sky's bodies burned down.

Cimil winked. "I have a few in my basement for emergencies. Never know when you'll need a spare."

Odd, but maybe Willa could work with this. She was certain she could win over Cimil. *Better to have her in my corner than working against me.* Such a powerful goddess could be an asset.

"All right." Willa stood and held out her hand. "I agree. I'll turn your vampire human, and you'll give the beast his own body. From there, we'll start doing whatever you need."

Cimil smiled, and they shook. "I'll be in touch in a few days."

Cimil left, and Willa went to the magic box. "Hello, I would like some spirits. Have anything with bubbles? I'm in the mood to celebrate."

Once she had the beast, she could take Damien out herself. *Bastard left me to die.*

CHAPTER TWENTY-ONE

MF and Maxton had arrived last night at her apartment with the two demons in tow. She'd microwaved a mac-n-cheese bowl and put on the TV for Maxton while she went to shower. She'd gone with a documentary on sharks, thinking he might enjoy all the chum scenes. But when she'd come out of the bathroom, Maxton was already passed out on the bed with the two demons.

"Bonbon! Gorgonzolina! What did I say about draining guests?"

"You said no customers from the store. He's not a customer," Bonbon had replied.

Gorgonzolina had licked her chops. "He tastes pretty dry anyway. Not much love inside him."

"I know you guys are tired after draining him on the plane. Swallowing down all that nasty witch's magic probably wasn't easy. But like I said before, if you guys are really hungry, you just have to ask. I'm happy to cuddle." MF had lain down next to Maxton and patted the side of the bed away from him. The two demons had hopped up, and she curled around them, stroking their soft little ears.

"Fuck yeah," Bonbon had moaned. "You touch those ears, you dirty girl. Harder. Like you mean it."

Gorg just purred like a kitten, as usual.

"You guys…are…weird…" MF had dosed off, the energy draining from her body.

Now it was late morning, and she felt something on her cheek.

MF slapped it away and opened her eyes. "Wha-what!"

"It is just me, Maxton." He sat on the edge of the bed.

"What are you doing?"

"Watching you sleep. I think your friends took advantage of you last night, so I decided to let you rest."

Gorg and Bon were both snoring away on the couch.

"Yeah, they do that occasionally. I strongly recommend never sleeping next to them."

"Agreed. I woke up with quite the headache." His eyes floated to her neck.

He was hungry? Actually, she was, too. She'd been so tired last night that she forgot about her dinner.

"Maxton, I haven't eaten since yesterday morning. I can't donate blood right now. I'm really sorry. Think you can wait?"

He took her hand and kissed her wrist.

Was he going to bite her against her will? She

was about to jerk her arm away when he began trailing soft kisses up her arm.

"What are you doing?" she asked, her breathing accelerating.

"I woke up next to you with a *different* sort of hunger."

Wait. Is he... "Are you coming on to me?"

"If you mean trying to persuade you to let me bed you, then yes."

Her heart began beating faster. "But I thought you didn't like me that way."

"You thought wrong."

Yeah, maybe she had. On one hand, she had hoped their two moments yesterday meant something to him, but she didn't want to behave like a naïve human. She knew perfectly well that vampires used seduction to get their meals.

He added, "I find you thoroughly interesting, Mountain Flower." He brushed a lock of hair from her face. "And very beautiful. I would like to explore what might happen if I took off your clothes," he leaned over and kissed her collarbone, "and then removed my clothes," another kiss up her neck, sending shivers down her spine, "and then inserted my rather generous penis in your—"

"Okay. I get the picture."

"Have I insulted you? You are not a virgin, correct?"

"No. I'm an ex-vampire and happen to still have the libido of one." She bowed her head, trying to capture his gaze. "But how do I know you're not just saying all this because you want to drink from me?"

"Oh," he grinned, "I want to drink from you. The question is, do you want to drink from me?"

Her mouth dropped. "Are you offering to—"

"To turn you."

"What-what changed your mind?" she asked.

He sat up straight, captivating her with his intense, lustful stare. "You have been transparent with me, so I shall do the same for you. I do not know what changed my mind. I woke up, saw you there, and felt empathy for the first time in a very long while. Perhaps it is because you stopped me from making a grave mistake last night. Maybe it is because you have shown a fearless warmth and compassion for a man who does not deserve it. All I know is that I felt the urge to do something for you in return. While also putting my generous penis in your vag—"

"Sex. We can just say sex." MF exhaled slowly. So this was it. Her last day as a human. And she was going to be turned by a man she strongly believed was her mate.

A) Her instant attraction.

B) He gave her a big fat "O-my" without killing her when taking blood.

C) He figured out what her name really meant.

D) She stopped his rampage with a kiss.

E) He woke up this morning wanting to give

her the D! And the B!

These were all signs.

"Then I will say it, MF. I would like to have sex and offer you my blood."

She wanted to cry. Pure tears of joy. "Can I eat first?"

He tilted his head. "Eat?"

"Yeah. I never got the chance to say goodbye to all my favorite foods the first time around. I'd like to do this right. In fact, you can help me."

"Help?"

"I have a lot of favorite foods."

"How many?" he asked.

"That's right. You've never been to a grocery store. Get ready for one of my favorite pastimes, besides sex: snacking."

He laughed. "I am thoroughly intrigued by your depraved whims, Mountain Flower. Show me this dark store of repulsive *grosseries*. If it's as terrifying as the moving vomit-sleigh you showed me last evening, I am in for quite the ride."

ॐ ∽

"Where the hell is MF when I need her?" Damien paced his bedroom while Sky bawled her eyes out inconsolably, facedown on his bed. She'd been like this for hours. He'd attempted to hold her, talk calmly, ply her with powerful apple-tinis, and he'd even gone out and bought two dozen doughnuts.

Which he'd ended up stress eating. Nothing soothed the woman, who refused to say a word.

"Sky, please talk to me. Tell me what I must do to stop you from crying."

She lifted her head, flashing a set of insanely puffy eyes, before burying her face in his wet pillow again.

Dear gods. These weren't the fake sobs meant to extract sympathy either. She was having a genuine meltdown. Every muscle in her body shook with despair, trying to dispel the overflow of sadness.

He began getting teary eyed, too. It was unnatural to watch a living creature suffer so deeply and not feel anything.

"Sky, I need you to stop this," he said tenderly. "If you could simply listen, then perhaps I could—"

"Go away! Just die! I hate you!"

Ah. Finally. She said words. This is good. "Yes. You hate me. Say more. Tell me what you are feeling." He waved his hand in a circle.

She sat up, a human ball of snot and tears. "You did this to me. You fucking…you fucking," she hiccuped, "you showed up in my life. Uninvited."

Not invited by her. It had been Cimil's doing. "As I explained before, Cimil blackmailed me into working for her. She demanded I find you. But I swear, if I had to do it all over again, I would."

Sky snarled at him. "Gah! You are so evil!"

"Sorry. Sorry. I did not mean I wouldn't change things—such as running you over. I merely meant I wouldn't change meeting you, Sky."

She pointed at him. "You're the devil! You and your slick tongue! You made me fall in love with you, all so you could sentence me to death again. Only now I know what's waiting for me on the other side. It's not the end. It's just the beginning of an eternity of humiliation, of knowing you chose someone else when I chose you!" She began bawling again. "You don't deserve me!"

She turned over, screaming into the pillow, "Go away, Damien! Leave me alone."

All right. That was enough. He'd been sitting here for hours trying to soothe her. All he wanted to do was discuss the facts. With honesty. The only way he knew how to be with Sky. He hoped she might help him find a way out of this mess because, honestly, Sky was the smartest person he'd ever known.

"Enough!" he roared and grabbed her from the bed.

"Stop it. What are you doing?" She kicked and screamed.

He held her tightly by the waist from behind, dragging her to his bathroom.

"Let me go, you nasty bitch!" she yelled.

"I am not a bitch." Nasty was debatable. "I am through with your pity party." He pulled her into the shower and turned it on. Cold water.

The ceiling showerhead rained on them both, and she screamed. "That's fucking cold!"

"Yeah! I know." He held her tight so she couldn't let go. "And when you calm the hell down, I'll turn it off. Until then, scream away. This entire home was built by a very sadistic vampire. Scream-proof!"

Sky kicked and clawed at his arms, but he'd had worse. As a fixer, he used to torture people to get information he could use for his clients. As an assassin he'd done the same. No, he wasn't proud of it, but facts were facts.

After a minute, she realized she wasn't getting free.

"Fine. I'll stop," she said. "Just turn off the water, please."

"You promise no more crying?"

She nodded, and he released her. She turned around in his arms and looked up at him with her big bloodshot eyes.

His heart sagged in his chest. She was right. He'd done this to her.

He gazed deeply into her eyes, seeing the woman underneath who captivated him from the first moment they met. "You were wearing sweats with pizza stains," he said.

"What?"

"When I met you."

"You mean when you broke into my house?" she asked.

He toggled his head. "I was doing a wellness check." He'd come to her home to ask some questions about a fairy sighting, but the place looked like it had been unoccupied for a while. "And you looked very well. You still do."

"Don't, Damien. Don't start with me."

"But you started it by saying you love me," he pointed out.

"Yes, but you don't love me back."

He shook his head. "That is where you are wrong. I was going to drive away that day we met. And maybe I should've. But I couldn't. I saw something in your eyes, and it grabbed hold."

She blinked up at him. "What's it matter now? It was all for nothing. All of it."

He reached around her, hit the setting for his usual warm shower, and started unbuttoning his shirt.

"What are you doing?" she asked.

"Taking a shower." He stripped off his pants and got naked.

Sky glanced down at his erection. "Do you normally have that when you bathe?"

He leaned down and kissed her softly. She kissed him back, her soft lips moving with his.

"Wait." She pulled away. "We can't do this, Damien."

"Why not?" He was naked. She could be naked too with a little effort.

"Because you're just going to turn around afterwards and sentence me to die."

"All I know for certain is that I don't want to

lose you, Sky. You are the one I want. But that doesn't mean I want Willa to die." He kept hoping he'd find a way to talk Cimil out of this ridiculous, cruel game.

Sky drew a breath. "Do you love me?"

Damien knew he did, but admitting it also felt like sentencing her to death. "Bad things happen to the people I care for, Sky. You know that firsthand."

"If I'm going to die by the end of the day, then I deserve to hear the truth."

Tell her, you pussy. Tell her and then fuck her and then kill her.

Damien wanted to tell the beast to fucking die already, but it was pointless. He was never going to leave or change.

"Sky, I do love you. Deeply. And I regret that it might not be enough."

She stroked his wet cheek. "Thank you for the truth." She kissed him hard and then left him in the shower alone.

Damien felt like he was being torn in two. Why was he so intent on saving Willa when he knew in his heart he was in love with Sky?

It makes no sense, he thought. *Why can't I let go of Willa?* The only answer he could come up with was his loyalty. Willa had died in his arms after losing the baby and being poisoned. Her final words to him were a curse, that he would be destined to live his life alone, and that the people around him would all die, too. Turned out not to be a curse but merely a fact. On her deathbed, she'd seen his future. So far, she'd been right.

Maybe that was the root of it all. He believed if he chose Sky, she'd die anyway, and it would be his fault again.

Letting Cimil do the deed was the easy way out.

He exhaled sharply. "I know what I must do." He was ready to choose.

CHAPTER TWENTY-TWO

"You were not making light when you called that store gross. Why do humans consume things that nature did not provide?" Maxton stared at MF's counter cluttered with all the bad stuff—ice cream, doughnuts, cookies, potato salad, those mini pizzas she loved, and a ton of candy.

"Because they taste delicious." She patted her stomach. "And I'm full."

"You only had a few bites."

"Of fifteen different things." She smiled, staring at Maxton's large frame in her kitchen.

"Why are you looking at me like that?"

She shrugged coyly. "I just like seeing you here in my apartment." She liked seeing him in her life, too.

"Well, do not get used to it."

MF tilted her head. "Why? Where are you thinking we should go after tonight?"

He gave her a stern look. "I am returning to my lair."

"Maxton," she laughed, "I'm not going to live

in some damp muddy cave in the middle of no-where. Plus, I can't abandon Damien and the demons. Not without finding a replacement, and even then, they're my friends. I'd like to see them once in a while."

"I am sorry if I gave you the wrong impression, MF, but I did not mean that as an invitation."

MF jerked her head back. "Wait. You're-you're just planning to turn me and go?"

"Did you think I would remain here in this cesspool of a city to enjoy the scent of stale human urine in the air? Or the constant noise?"

She couldn't argue with that, but he wasn't even willing to take her with him. Not that she'd go, but still. "I don't know what to say."

Maxton took her hand. "Do not look so disap-pointed, MF. I have agreed to change you. Is that not what you wanted?"

She blinked. Suddenly, she wasn't so sure. "If you go home, I'll be all alone."

"You have your friends, as you just said."

But that wasn't the same as being turned by an ancient vampire who could truly teach her to be the best damned vampire ever. One who had complete control over her urges and powers. Without Max-ton, it would be like reliving the nightmare from the first turning.

MF swallowed hard. "I need time to think, Stewart."

"Stewart?"

She shook her head from side to side. "Sorry. I meant Maxton."

"Who is Stewart?"

"The first selfish bastard who turned me and left. Guess I confused you with him for a second in my head." She drew a breath. "I'll get you a ride to Damien's."

"You want me to leave? But what about putting my pen—"

"No. No sex. And I need time to think things through."

"Do not wait too long, MF. I only have until the end of the day."

"What are you talking about?" MF frowned.

He pulled a piece of paper from his pocket. "Go ahead. Look."

She took it and unfolded the paper. On it was a list of names written in pink crayon. Her name was at the top. "What is this?"

"I am not at liberty to say, but you are a smart woman. Figure it out."

She didn't know Cimil's handwriting, but who else would write a list in crayon and give it to a vampire? "It's Cimil's kill list."

He shook his head no.

Not a kill list. "Why else would she give you a list? It can't be another one of her orgies. Her kids are on…that…list." MF's mouth dropped. "It's a turn list, isn't it?" So that was why he'd had a change of heart about turning her.

Anger and betrayal spiked through her. "Why, Maxton? Why pretend you liked me? Why make me think I was special? If all you wanted was to turn me so you get whatever Cimil's offered you, you could've just been honest." MF was beyond hurt.

"I did not look at the list until we were at the gross place. I swear it, MF."

Deceitful, lying, manipulative vampire! She pointed at the door. "Get out. Just get out."

"But, MF, I—"

"Whatever she's offering you, you're not getting it with my help. Go back to your jungle, Maxton. Go back to your lonely cave." She opened her door. "Oh look. It's nice and sunny out." *Good. Let him suffer in the heat.* "You can wait out there for your taxi."

Maxton walked out, head raised high, and she slammed the door behind him.

I'm so sick of this bullshit! Cimil had her hands in all the pies.

First she'd told MF that her destiny was being a vampire, and she had to work with Damien to get her life back on track. Then MF had found out there was only one vampire left in the world. *And he's a smokin' hot turd! With a penchant for killing innocent people!* Then she fell for him anyway, misreading all the signs like a chump!

I felt something. I honestly did. But he couldn't be her mate. He wasn't into her. The only reason he was being nice was to check her name off Cimil's list.

MF's stomach churned. "Why did I eat all the crap?"

⌘ ⌘

Damien was heading out the door to go see Cimil when Maxton walked in, looking wilted.

"What happened to you?" Damien asked.

"I need blood. The damned ride here nearly killed me." Maxton went to Damien's kitchen and looked out the back door. "Do you have any squirrels or rabbits here?"

Damien followed him. "No. I do not. But the UPS guy generally shows up around this time. Are you proficient at erasing memories?"

Maxton turned around, flustered. "She kicked me out. Can you believe it? I offered to give the damned woman what she wanted, and she kicked me out. I then stepped in a puddle of urine. This entire cesspool of LA is covered in human piss!"

"Part of the charm. Also, that piss you stepped in wasn't human. MF has an ongoing rivalry with Big Foot."

"What the devil is a Big Foot?" Maxton barked.

"Never mind. Just tell me what happened. Is MF all right?"

"She is a cantankerous, pious, judgmental, blathering human female. That is what she is."

"So you had a disagreement. About what?" Damien asked, trying not to laugh. It was amusing to see this vampire's manly parts in a twist over MF.

"I cannot tell you because it will void my arrangement with Cimil."

Cimil strikes again. Why am I not surprised? Seemed the goddess was busy ruining all sorts of lives lately. "Well, say no more, then. I am on my way to see her now, if you'd like to have a word."

"Are you going to tell her your choice?" Maxton asked.

Damien nodded.

"Very good. I will come with you and do the same."

The doorbell rang. "What was that?" Maxton asked.

"Your snack."

"Just in time. I was considering knocking on your neighbor's door."

Damien shook his head and went to get his package. "By the way, you didn't happen to go to an amusement park last night, did you?"

"Why?" Maxton asked, looking guiltier than sin.

"The security cameras recorded someone who looks like you making out with someone who looks like MF, in front of children. Pretty sick."

"Was not me."

CHAPTER TWENTY-THREE

Driving his red convertible Mustang with the top up for Maxton—*Grrrr*—Damien called ahead to ensure Cimil was home to receive his reply, but Roberto said she was out.

"Thank you, Your Majesty," Damien said politely, since Roberto was still technically a king. "Please tell her to call me. I will be at my shop. It is most urgent I speak to her."

"She has been MIA all day. If you see her before I do," Roberto grumbled, "let her know I wish to speak with her, too. I have my answer."

Cimil had given an ultimatum to her husband, also? Interesting how everyone's answers were due by end of day today. *What is she up to?*

Damien changed course and headed for Greystone and Sons to wait for Cimil to magically show up. He needed to open the store anyway. There was a long line of grumpy customers anxious to pick up their alterations.

Damien pulled into his spot at the back and parked. "Maxton, I have a dark storeroom with a cot. You can sleep there if you like. I'll wake you when Cimil shows up."

"Very good." They entered, and he showed Maxton where to take his nap. Damien then flipped on the lights, turned on the soft classical music—a little Chopin—and opened up the front.

Ah, how I missed you, shop. His sanctuary. His slice of civilized, manly respite.

The front door chimed. "You won't fucking believe what he did, Damien!" MF stormed in, wearing torn jeans, those God-awful military boots, and a frilly Victorian-style top with a high neck. Sleeves torn off.

Sanctuary no more. "MF, I presume you are here to vent about Maxton, but—"

"That lying, manipulative, fucking vampire? You bet your ass! He offered to turn me this morning. Did you know that? And here I was, Damien, thinking he was my mate, that there was some sort of divine love for me in the universe. But no. He just wanted to make Cimil happy by turning me along with a long list of other names. Can you believe that crap?"

"You thought he was your mate?" When had this happened? Why didn't she say something? He'd almost killed Maxton.

"Well, yeah. All the signs were there. He sucked my blood, and I came so hard that I forgot my name. And when he totally lost his shit last night, after vomiting out his guts from the roller-coaster ride, I stopped his hangry rampage. He came this close," she held up her thumb and forefinger, "to snacking on some kids. But then I kissed him, pulled him out of it, and fed him."

So Maxton lied. Did the tough, fearless vampire feel embarrassed about having feelings for MF? It was the only conclusion.

"But you say he's not actually your mate?" Damien asked.

"No. He was just putting on the charm the entire time, making me think he liked me." MF pressed her palm to her forehead. "I'm such an idiot, Damien. A bona fide bonehead. I really thought he was the one." She sighed. "But I guess I got what I deserved. I mean, what was I thinking? I should've known better than to buy his act. It was exactly the same way Stewart Hedgeworth lured me to his hotel room."

Damien did not like the sound of this story. Mostly because he knew it would end in a very ugly place. "I am sure it was very traumatic, MF. And it is something you should leave in the past." *Please say no more. I have endured enough drama this morning.*

"I have. Mostly. But how can I ever forget? I was just this naïve, sweet young woman wanting to break free from my parents and see the world. No more hemp weaving. No more organic apples and canning jams. No more chickens and eggs and lavender sachets. Sure, they were making millions with their all-organic brands, and yes, I stood to inherit it all, but that wasn't the life I dreamed of for myself. Then along comes this dark, seductive, exotic creature of the night, promising to show me the world and love me forever. All I had to do was hand myself over to him. And I did, Damien. I fell for his spiel. Hook, line, and sinker."

"Wait. Did you just say you inherited your family's multimillion-dollar enterprise?"

"Yes. Marv and Mary's Organics. I ran their hemp clothing division. Mostly my designs, but eventually I had to hire help and just focus on the business."

Damien's jaw slacked. He was not into organics, but this brand was on every shelf, in every supermarket. There was even a shop downtown dedicated to their organic clothing.

"You told me your parents were poor hippies and made you sew your own clothes. That was how you learned."

MF shrugged. "All true. Except for the poor part. They died very rich."

"You said you were homeless."

"And I was. I'd just sold my townhouse, wanting to upgrade to a house closer to the farm, when that vampire killed my folks. And after what happened, I couldn't live at their place. Eventually, I sold it along with the company."

"For how much?" Not that it mattered, but she'd been portraying the down-and-out lost child.

"I don't know. A lot, I guess. I gave some to

charity. But that's not the point. I should've kept the company. I should've taken it over and guarded their legacy. But I was just too devastated over losing them. And it was all my fault, Damien. If only I hadn't trusted Stewart. But I did. And here I am, falling for the same bullshit again." MF sighed. "I am a stupid human."

"You are not stupid, MF." He put his hand on her shoulder.

"Then why did I trust a vampire again?" she snapped.

"You tell me."

"Because I wanted it so badly. I thought if I lived long enough and worked really hard, I could buy back my parents' company and do right by them. That's why when Cimil said being a vampire was my destiny, I trusted her."

Damien couldn't believe his ears. Here was this young woman he believed was a nomadic misfit, but she was really an heiress. *California is so confusing. People who dress like they're homeless but are worth millions, and people who dress like they're worth millions but are bankrupt.*

MF's eyes started tearing as she turned for the door.

"You're leaving?" Damien asked.

"I just came by to drop off the demons. They overate, so don't let them in the dressing rooms."

"Where are you going?" Damien asked.

"To visit my parents' grave. I have to tell them I

failed." MF opened the door and returned quickly with the demon stroller. "Here you go, boss." She kissed her fingertips and pressed them to each demon's sleeping face. "You guys are awesome little demons with really good hearts. Don't let anyone tell you otherwise. Be good."

MF left.

"That fucking prick. I'll tear his dick off." Maxton appeared behind Damien, fists balled.

"Are you all right?" Because MF did not have a dick. Not that Damien had checked, but it was the sort of thing a tailor noticed. Bulges had to be accounted for.

"No," Maxton snarled.

"I'm sure MF will get over your falling-out, Maxton. She is not the sort of woman to give up on life because of a man. And she is no threat to you, so best to leave her genitals alone."

"I meant that I am going to kill Stewart Hedgeworth." Maxton narrowed his eyes into hateful orbs.

"Stewart? The one who killed MF's family? You know him?"

Maxton nodded, his green eyes turning black.

"How?"

"I sired him. And he is why I moved to the jungle."

CHAPTER TWENTY-FOUR

Damien wanted to follow Maxton when he'd left, but just as the vampire exited in a fierce rage, four customers showed up looking to claim their alterations. MF had already gone to the cemetery to visit her departed parents.

And shortly, I must tell Cimil my choice. One that he would regret for as long as he lived. He suspected that was what the sadistic goddess wanted all along: to create despair. She used it to divide people, only to come up with a plan to rescue them all. *Kind of like politicians.*

The funny part was how everyone kept falling for it. Even him. She created the crisis, and then, after whipping everyone into an emotional frenzy, she presented a solution. That solution generally resulted in more concessions for her. *More power.*

He had to stop her. But how?

The only ones capable were the other gods, and they were out of the picture. Or were they?

Damien grabbed his cell and dialed Brutus.

"Hello?" Brutus's deep voice came over the line.

"Brutus, Damien here. I need to get a hold of Votan, the God of Death and War."

～ ～

Votan was sitting on his dock, overlooking the turquoise waters of Lake Bacalar in Mexico, with a fishing pole in his hand. Emma, his sweet wife, was still asleep after a long night of lovemaking. The kids were back in New York with Emma's family.

Ah, how I love this time of day. Everything was peaceful and quiet. No more godding and drama to worry about. *Deity retirement is incredible.* After seventy thousand years of fighting wars, he'd never been happier.

His sat phone suddenly vibrated in his pocket. "Dammit. This'd better be important." Hopefully the children were all right.

He looked at the caller ID. The number was from LA. "Hello?"

"Votan. Damien Greystone here. I apologize for the intrusion, but there is an urgent matter."

Votan wondered if this had something to do with the Great Explosion. Before the gods had hung up their togas, they agreed to hire him to investigate what had happened. Mostly to determine if there was a way to bring back the supernatural lives that had been lost.

"What is the problem?" Votan said.

"Cimil. She needs to be stopped."

Cimil? But she was supposed to be retired, too. "What is she up to now?"

"Wreaking havoc on our lives. That's what."

Votan really did not want to deal with yet another Cimil situation. "Have you spoken to K'ak, the new God of the Underworld?"

Votan wasn't sure if Damien Greystone knew that the gods had changed roles right before shutting down operations. It was a long story, having to do with him and his brethren being forced to travel through a demon portal after being trapped by the demon king. Demon portals were wonky like that.

It all worked out fine in the end, he supposed, since the gods no longer needed their powers, but Cimil had become the God of Death and War. Votan was now the God of Love, and so on. Again, no one really cared because they'd retired. All except K'ak, who was supposed to be on point, since someone needed to keep in touch with the Uchben and look after the Underworld. However, even he was not allowed to meddle in the lives of the humans anymore. It was law. They'd all agreed.

"K'ak?" Damien said. "Never met him."

"He doesn't wear clothing, so he probably never came in for fitting, but he should have reached out. Are you certain he hasn't checked in on your investigation regarding the Great Explosion? Tall fellow. Long dark hair with silver streaks? Very naked."

"No. When did he take Cimil's role?"

"Never mind." Votan paused, trying to figure out what was going on.

Damien added, "Cimil is the only deity I've spoken with recently, and she pulled me off that case—said there was nothing more to be done. At the moment, she has me working on reviving the vampire race."

What! Votan's blood boiled. He should've known that Cimil wouldn't stop meddling. "Anything else?"

"Normally, I do not believe in tattling, but I feel this situation calls for an exception."

"Go on, tailor. Tell me everything."

CHAPTER TWENTY-FIVE

Maxton absolutely hated the modern world except for one thing: Human "technology" made it fairly easy to locate someone. All he had to do was ask the "cell" (a magical device), as Maxton's yellow automobile driver had done ("Where do I find this Stewart T. Hedgeworth, the vampire?"). And then plunkitty-plunk! The answer was pulled from thin air and displayed in the man's hand.

Amazing. Maxton wondered what else he might find by asking the man's shiny rectangle.

Stewart lived three hours from the LA city, in a town called *Tee-who-anna*. The ruffian had miraculously settled down and opened an establishment called Vampiro Stewart's, where—according to the driver—young people listened to music, danced, and found partners for "getting busy."

Maxton understood this to mean that they fornicated out of wedlock. Sounded enjoyable enough, but Maxton knew from experience that nothing Stewart did had respectable intentions. Wasn't in his nature.

Maxton straightened his blood red tie and entered the place, taking in the odd decor—a coffin in the corner, black-velvet-upholstered furniture, and a set of fangs the size of an elephant stuck to the wall.

A vampire den? Obviously, it was only made to look like one, but why would Stewart be advertising his species, even going so far as to reveal himself on the placard above the exterior doorway?

Then Maxton realized something. *Stewart is human again.* He was aggrandizing his past.

Stewart appeared through a narrow door in the back, holding a box of bottles. "Hey, we're closed. We open at ten tonight..." Stewart's beady eyes met Maxton's.

"Hello, Stewart."

"Master?" Stewart fumbled with the box, nearly dropping it. "I mean *Maxton.* What-what're you doing here? I thought you were dead. The undead kind of dead, I mean."

"No. I am quite well."

"What do you want?" Stewart's voice trembled, like the weak slithering snake that he was.

"I have come for dance lessons."

Stewart stared, his thin lips smashed together.

"Fool. I am here to settle old scores."

Stewart set the box on the table to his side. "Look, man. It was a long, long time ago. We're not even vamps anymore. Why don't we just shake hands and let bygones be bygones? We both did things we aren't proud of, yeah?"

Maxton smiled wickedly. "Oh, do not worry, friend. I am not here because you killed my wife and child. I blame myself for that." It had been Maxton's foolish decision to turn Stewart, an event that happened well before Maxton would meet Lou Ellen.

Lou Ellen had been a kind person with a pure heart. It was the reason Maxton spared her life instead of drinking her to death on that fateful night hundreds of years ago.

Weeks later, he would run into her again and warn her about being out alone so late at night. She explained how she'd been widowed recently and had a daughter, Mable. During the day, they worked in a kitchen for a wealthy family, but it wasn't enough money. So at night, Lou Ellen worked for the town baker, making bread. She was saving to start a new life elsewhere for her and her child.

After that, Maxton began checking on Lou Ellen and Mable, and they formed a friendship. Eventually, Maxton would confess he was a vampire, but Lou Ellen did not care. She convinced him to turn his back on his violent vampire ways and find God. It was why he became a Catholic and a peaceful vampire. A married vampire. With a human daughter he claimed as his own. They were happy, though Maxton always feared his past would catch up to him.

And it did.

The three were living outside of Rome, running

their own bakery, when Maxton ran into Stewart one evening. Stewart had become a violent, blood-thirsty sonofabitch, and Maxton tried to convince him to find a new way. Like a prideful fool, he brought Stewart home to meet Lou Ellen and Mable—proof of his moral accomplishment.

Stewart had laughed in his face and left.

The next night, Stewart returned while Maxton was out, and killed Lou Ellen and Mable. Finding their lifeless bodies broke something deep inside Maxton, causing him to break his vow to God to never kill again. Killing seemed to be the only thing that took the pain away while he hunted Stewart. But the vile monster was nowhere to be found, and over time, Maxton grew to understand how he alone had triggered the events. Vampires were abominations. End of story.

"So, how you wanna do this? Fists? Guns?" Stewart reached for something behind him. "I like guns."

"They will be of no use to you, Stewart, because I remain a vampire. And you, my old friend, have penance to pay. Then I'm going to turn you inside out like an old stocking."

Maxton smiled and flashed his fangs.

༚ ༚

That night, MF was watching her favorite vampire movie, *What We Do in the Shadows,* curled up next to a box of tissues. It was going to take a long time to get over her idiocy—trusting a stupid vampire! *Gah! What was I thinking?*

At least she knew if her parents were still alive, they would forgive her. They had never been the type of people to expect perfection or demand that others follow their philosophies of life. They simply did their thing.

"Mountain Flower, there are only two types of people in this world," her father used to say. "Good or bad. Nothing else matters. Not if they agree with you or like you. It doesn't even matter if you have absolutely nothing in common or you're on opposite sides of the political spectrum. If they're good, you treat them with the respect they deserve. If they're bad, you keep your distance."

But above all, her parents always taught her to forgive. "Especially the good, Mountain Flower," Mom would say. "Good people must be allowed to make mistakes. It's how we all learn to become better people."

MF sighed. "If only I could forgive myself." She'd made the biggest mistake of her life, and then she failed to learn from it. *Why did I trust a vampire again?* She'd honestly started falling in love with him, too. *Idiot!*

There was a loud scratch on her door. "Oh, fuck off, Big Foot! Get a life!"

"It is I, Maxton. Open up."

Maxton? Why the hell was he back? "Sorry, MF

isn't home right now. This is her virtual assistant—a very new invention that stupid, crusty old vampires don't know about. Because they're stupid."

"Nice try, woman. I can smell you in there. Now open up, or I will destroy this door."

"Ugh!" She hopped up and jerked open the door. "I told you to leave…" MF jumped back, her eyes zeroing in on a face that had haunted her every night since her family died. "What the hell?"

Maxton stepped in, pushing her aside and dragging that piece of trash with him.

She shut the door behind them, her heart beating with the sort of rage a person felt when left to stew and stew and stew some more.

MF's fists clenched. "What is this, Maxton?" Stewart wasn't talking or moving much. He wasn't tied up either. He was just standing there staring at her floor like a zombie.

"I have come to make things right." Maxton raised his chin.

"By bringing this murdering piece of dog crap into my home?"

"As you see, I come with an apology. And no, I did not mean to rhyme just now. Purely a coincidence."

"Noted. But how did you even find out about him?" she asked.

"I was at Damien's shop earlier, in the storeroom."

He'd overheard her rant. "So you went and

found the vampire who killed my family? Why?"

"I am the reason he exists, which means I am the reason you lost your family. And my own. It is why I went on a rampage lasting years, committing vile acts I hardly recall. It is why, in a moment of what I believe was divine intervention, I stopped the bloodshed and exiled myself."

Okay. This was a lot to take in. "You're saying that you made Stewart into a vampire. And he killed your family?"

"Yes. My human wife and adopted daughter."

MF covered her mouth. "I'm so sorry, Maxton. That's awful." How did she not know he had a family once? "But you can't blame yourself. Not for that or for what happened to my family."

"Then who? Who gets the blame?" he grumbled.

"For starters," she pointed to Stewart, "that guy right there."

"I taught him everything he knows—how to lure, seduce, hunt, and kill."

"Okay. But you were trying to be a good maker. I bet you even taught him the difference between good and bad people so he'd choose his victims properly. Right? What he did with that information was his call. Not yours."

"Well, yes. I suppose," Maxton said.

"And I bet he liked the taste of the rotten apples, like any normal vampire would. Just as nature intended." It was simply a fact that bad people tasted better.

"I do not know what nature intended, but yes," Maxton replied. "Stewart was shown the culinary delights of dining on evil mortals."

"See. There you go. You taught him how to be a good vampire, and he still chose to be a dirty, murderous piece of shit. That's on him, Maxton. Not you." MF exhaled, trying to let it all sink in. Maxton had made the vampire who changed her life. Even stranger was that she'd been turned by Maxton's progeny, which meant she'd once belonged to Maxton's bloodline. *Whoa. Is that why I feel so connected to him?*

"I'm so sorry about your family. I really am." She sighed.

"And I am sorry about yours." Maxton looked away, flustered.

"Thanks, but why are you here? With him?" She glanced at Stewart, noting how small and pathetic he looked. In her mind, she'd built him up to be a ten-foot-tall monster with great powers. *He's just a slimy little man.*

"First, I intend to dismember Stewart in your honor," Maxton replied. "Then I plan to…" His voice faded. Maxton blinked and then blinked some more, like he was trying to figure something out. "From there, I will leave it up to you." His green eyes locked on her face.

"Leave what?"

"Regardless of Stewart, I have done plenty to

deserve living in a damp muddy cave for eternity. But you are a good woman, MF. You remind me of my Lou Ellen, my first and only true friend. And if she were here today, I know she would tell me two things: One, to forgive myself, which will never happen. And two, to seek redemption. This I can do. So, if your destiny is to become a vampire, then I am obligated to put aside my life and ensure you are the best damned vampire ever. Good people make good vampires. Great people make really great vampires."

MF gasped. That was exactly how she felt!

Maxton went on, "If I want to truly pay penance for my actions, it is not enough to sit in the jungle—sweating, getting dirty, eating tiny innocent animals day after day. I must go where I'm needed. I must support you, MF—a shining example of all things good."

Her eyes teared. Suddenly, deep in her heart, she knew she hadn't made a mistake. He was the one. A *good* one, too.

"Do you still wish to be turned?" he asked.

MF looked at her watch. It was almost midnight. "What about Cimil's list?"

"If I am to be by your side, becoming mortal defeats the purpose." Maxton glanced at Stewart. "As for him, you will need a hearty meal once you wake a vampire. He will be quite tasty. Better than the gross food from the gross store."

MF smiled.

CHAPTER TWENTY-SIX

MF felt like her insides were unraveling with excitement, fear, and all the things that came with ending one's life and beginning another. *Talk about a roller coaster.*

This morning she had been in love, ready to go all in. By midday she had been heartbroken and accepted the fact she'd never get the chance to do right by her parents. Now, at nearly midnight, Maxton had proven her wrong about everything.

The weirdest part was when she sat in front of her family's graves today, sobbing uncontrollably about being such a letdown, MF could've sworn something poked her in the ass, as if to say, "Get up, girl. You have work to do."

Maxton emerged from the shower with a towel around his waist, his prominent pecs and sex-pack glistening with water.

Damn. What I wouldn't give to wash my panties on his washboard abs. Of course, she'd still be wearing said panties.

Sitting on her bed in just her black robe, MF

swallowed a lump in her throat. "How are you feeling?" He was about to turn her. Was he excited, too?

"I feel incredible. These modern showers are a marvel after centuries of bathing in a muddy river filled with leaches and piranha. And these pomades for the hair and your soap? I have never felt my exterior so well moisturized."

MF grinned. So the vampire liked showers, natural conditioner, and very nice suits—all things she could make happen. *Just wait until he sees my sewing.* She could construct a tux like no other.

"Are you ready?" Maxton asked, tossing back his wet hair.

She nodded. "A little nervous, but yeah."

He sat next to her on the bed. "You know you do not have to become a vampire again in order to be magnificent. That goal has already been achieved."

She smiled, staring into his glittering eyes. "Thank you. But I want to do this." There was so much to do and so little time as a human. "Go on then." She tilted her head, brushing her long hair to one side.

Maxton didn't hold back, pushing his mouth to her neck while cupping the back of her head. His fangs went in as she fell back. He was immediately on top of her, stretched over her body.

MF started panting, unable to stop the need to struggle. In her heart, she wanted this, but her brain suddenly wanted to fight to live.

Just stay calm, she told herself.

Maxton drew on the wound, sucking and massaging.

First, she felt the tingle. Then came the throbbing. But she couldn't get her head in a quiet space.

"Stop. Stop. Wait."

Maxton broke away. "What is it?"

"Just…let me catch my breath."

Maxton brushed the hair from her forehead. "Take as long as you like, but do not ask me to start again unless you are certain, MF. I may not be able to stop myself next time."

She nodded, and he pressed his mouth to hers. His tongue slid against hers, his lips massaging skillfully, making her forget that she was about to die. Funny how he didn't taste like blood. He tasted like his scent—freshly cut cedar on a spring morning.

He slowly moved his body and nestled between her thighs, allowing her to feel his erection. *Christ, how I missed this.*

Had she mentioned that she'd never lost her vampire libido? MF went through more batteries than a cheap Christmas toy. *Thank gods I'll finally have a man who won't wear down after an hour.*

She slid her hands along his strong arms, around his tight narrow waist, and then up his muscled back. He was perfectly toned in all the right places.

His hand glided down between their bodies,

finding its way under her robe and between her thighs.

MF gasped the moment he teasingly stroked her C-spot with a featherlike touch—just enough pressure to make her want more. She moved her hips toward his hand, urging him to do it again.

Instead, he removed his towel and took his hard cock in his hand, positioning it at her entrance.

Her nipples pearled, and her skin tightened around her bones, goosebumps everywhere. But he still didn't penetrate, thrust, or give her the release she needed.

"Jesus, what are you doing?" she panted.

"Uh-uh-uh…no blaspheming." He circled the head of his shaft over her clit, drawing out the erotic pulses.

"Sorry. *Fuck*, what are you doing?" she said.

"Better." He sealed his mouth over hers, dipping the crown of his dick into her slick entrance. Then again. And again. Never going more than an inch. Or two inches, if she were measuring width.

"Stop teasing me."

"Tell me when to start," he said, his voice husky. "And I will start."

Shit. Shit! I'm ready. I want this. I want him. "Start."

He thrust deeply with the entire weight of his strong body, stealing her breath with his size. His fangs went in her neck.

"Oh gods. Oh gods." It felt like being fucked

fifteen different ways. Her body was tingling, pulsing, and throbbing inside and out. It was almost too much.

His hips moved like a piston, pounding in time with the pulling on her neck. MF felt her body heating and falling, preparing to explode in a giant ball of pleasure.

He hooked an arm under her knee, opening her wider for him. He thrust again, nailing her in that spot deep inside. *The C- and G-spot treatment. Yes...*

She rocked her hips, savoring his rapid breathing and guttural groans. Something about knowing he was lost in the moment and that she was the cause made it all so much fucking hotter.

He broke away from her neck and raised his head toward the ceiling, exposing his strong neck and Adam's apple. He was so beautiful. So purely male. So timelessly handsome. *I want nothing more.*

She started coming, throwing her head back, locking his legs with hers as the sinful pulses ripped through her core.

He groaned with pleasure, twitching inside her, coming too.

Suddenly, she felt something on her tongue. A drop of blood from his finger. She clamped her mouth around his finger and swallowed.

Her breathing slowed.

Her heart slowed.

Maxton withdrew his finger and kissed her again, tenderly lingering on her lips while he slowly pumped his cock in and out.

"Don't stop, Maxton," she muttered. She felt like she was floating in the sky. With a big dick between her legs. "This is definitely the way to be turned."

The room faded to black.

CHAPTER TWENTY-SEVEN

Damien called Cimil several times throughout the day, but she was nowhere to be found. Honestly, he was beginning to worry. After his conversation with Votan, Damien didn't know if the goddess had been taken or went into hiding.

Was her ultimatum still valid?

Just before midnight, Damien got a text to come outside his house. Strange because he didn't recognize the number.

He went out the front door and found Cimil behind the wheel of a white RV.

She honked the horn and waved him over.

Was this a trap? Did she know he'd gone to Votan for assistance? *Only one way to find out.*

He walked over and entered the RV through the side door. Cimil hopped out of the driver's seat.

"What is this place?" he asked, inspecting all of the lab equipment. At the far end, toward the back, was something resembling a tanning bed.

"Come and see this. You're going to love it." Cimil clapped excitedly.

He followed her over to the machine. "What does it do?"

"What doesn't it do? Now, get in, tailor."

"No." He stepped back.

"Look, cupcake, I don't have a lot of time here. 'Kay? This contraption is going to clean you up, spic and span, from the tippy top of your head down to your wiggly man toes."

"I have six showers. And a pool. I do not need help getting clean." Damien took another step back.

"Not that sort of clean." She poked his chest. "The sort of clean you've been wanting your entire life."

Hold on here. Do not get inside, brother. I sense she is up to something.

His beast was panicking like a wild animal bucking inside a cage. "Cimil, tell me what this is."

"This device will extract your beast."

"Excuse me?" Was she serious?

"Your beast. I'm going to remove it," Cimil said.

Do not do it! She means to kill me, brother!

"What do you plan to do with him?" Damien asked.

"Do you really care? In or out, tailor? Chop-chop. Because Minky says there is a gaggle of gods looking for me right now, and once they find me, this offer is done. Thank you for doing that, by the way. Votan is *pissssed*." She smiled.

"You know about that?"

"Uh, yeah. This whole retirement thing is ridiculous. They honestly believe that the world—that humans—no longer needs our intervention. Wrong! But since they won't listen to me, I have to show them. And you are going to help."

Damien was completely lost.

"Now get in the fucking chamber." Cimil narrowed her eyes. "Or I will have Minky stab your balls and shove 'em down your throat." Cimil raised the top half of the chamber.

Something to his right nudged him.

"What the...?" He jumped in place, but there was no one. *It's her damned Minky.*

Tailor! No! It is a trap. Do not do it!

Didn't matter what the beast said; if there was even a sliver of a chance that Cimil was telling the truth, Damien was doing this. *Free! No more fucking beast!* he thought.

Damien got inside the chamber and lay down. "By the way, I made my choice."

"Yes, yes. You choose Sky. I know." Cimil rolled her eyes.

"How?"

"You'll find out. Now close your eyes, because this is going to smart." Cimil closed the chamber.

Tailor! No! Let me out. We must fight!

A set of bright lights came on, flooding the chamber. Suddenly his body began to heat. He felt like he was burning up.

৵৵ ৵৵

Sky had given a lot of thought to the conversation with Damien earlier today. And after discussing things with her sister, Amelia, Sky had come to grips with the full weight and the reality of Damien's decision to choose only one woman.

She didn't envy him, but if Damien chose her, he needed to know the truth. She had a moral obligation to stop SBP. She would infiltrate them, just like Damien had suggested. She would gather information, find out who was really running things, and then she'd take them all out.

But that meant she had to cut herself off completely from everyone. For their own protection. *Is this how Damien felt when he broke things off with me?*

Because it sucked.

Especially because it could take years to get in deep with SBP. But if she could stop the testing, the mutilations, and the trafficking, she had to try. There was no one else coming to the rescue of these poor women and rare creatures. *Not many supernatural creatures left on the planet.*

Sky understood the urgency now more than ever. Because that article she wrote in Damien's name? Never saw the light of day. She'd arranged to publish it through an old contact at an independent news site known for its undercover work. But someone must've tipped off the governor because the site was shut down.

Going public with the story was a waste of time anyway. It was like Damien said, no one would believe her.

This was why she was going to talk to Damien. Sky wanted him to know her plan. If he'd chosen her, which he might've done already since it was almost midnight, he had to know she wasn't staying.

If he hadn't chosen her, and she was about to die, Sky wanted Damien to know that it changed nothing. She loved him and still would from beyond the grave. She needed him to understand that she forgave him and wouldn't haunt him this time so he could live his life with Willa.

In short, either way, this was goodbye. Also, she should probably return the Jag.

Sky pulled up to Damien's house behind a large white RV parked out front.

"What is this?" She squinted, trying to make out the small print over the bumper. "Property of SBP Enterprises?"

Oh crap. What are they doing here?

She hopped out of the Jag and cautiously approached. Just then, she spotted Bonbon, Gorgonzolina, and Pet coming out the front door.

"Hey, what's going on?" she asked.

"Don't know," Bonbon replied. "I was making sweet, sweet love to my lady here when we felt a disturbance in the demon force."

"What's the demon force?" Sky frowned.

"It's like in *Star Wars* but sticky," Gorgonzolina offered, as if that explanation were going to help.

"Why's it being disturbed? What's it mean?" Sky asked.

"Something powerful is very upset." Pet flew to the window of the trailer and looked inside. "Oh, look! A rage demon! Those are scary." She flew back into the house.

Pet saw something inside and didn't want to hump it? This couldn't be good. Pet wanted to hump everything—moving trains, trash cans, angry chipmunks.

"Bonbon, what the hell is a rage demon?" Sky asked.

"It is an unstoppable monster that thrives on torturing, killing, and doing pretty much anything else it can get away with that causes pain. So, basically like me, but nothing like me."

A seven-foot-tall man with long black hair and turquoise eyes walked up with another very tall man wearing tightie whities and holding a beer. "Has anyone seen a redheaded clown dressed as a woman?"

"Who are you?" Sky asked.

"Votan, God of Love. This is my brother Belch. Not sure what he's the god of anymore."

They were gods? Sky wasn't sure if the man was serious, but something about his hulking frame told her he wasn't here to fuck around. The guy in the underpants was a different story.

"I am guessing Cimil is inside?" Votan jerked his head toward the RV.

Sky shrugged.

Just then a taxi pulled up, and Willa hopped out wearing white leather pants and one of those gold and black Versace tops.

Willa sauntered up, clacking in her heels, looking bored. "Um," she flung her black hair over one shoulder, "I was in the middle of a massage and was summoned by Cimil. She told me to be here at midnight. What gives?"

Immediately, a silver minivan pulled up behind the Jag, and out climbed a very tall black man who looked like he was here to crack skulls.

"Votan. Belch." The man jerked his head at them. "My wife told me to meet her here. What the devil is going on? She's been avoiding me and the kids all day."

"Roberto, pleasure to see you again," said Votan. "Were you aware that Cimil has been meddling again?"

"She swore she was only keeping an eye on things, but not influencing. I figured it was harmless stuff, but today I found out she has an Instagram account with one billion followers. Also, she's been scheming to have me turned into a vampire again, along with our children. She threatened to leave me if I do not go along with it."

"Then she has broken the gods' law. She is in very big trouble," said Votan.

Sky was absolutely floored. So this was Cimil's husband. And he used to be a vampire? And these two huge dudes were actually gods?

The guy in the white underpants, Belch, chugged his beer and tossed the can over his shoulder. "I fucking knew it wouldn't last. And I was just getting really good at not drinking. Margarita's going to be pissed."

Sky had no idea what his story was, but it had to wait for another time. "Is someone going to do something about the rage demon inside the RV?"

"There's a rage demon? Inside there? With Cimil?" Roberto looked at Votan. "Well, fucking do something. I have no powers."

"What do you want me to do?" Votan replied. "Hug it into submission?"

"Don't look at me," said Belch. "I don't have a fucking clue what I'm doing anymore. Not since Colel took my powers and gave up her bees."

What the shit were these immortals talking about?

"Guys, where is Damien?" Sky asked Bonbon and Gorgonzolina.

Bonbon just stared, followed by a *woof!*

"Why are you talking to that tiny dog?" Votan asked.

"He's not a dog," said Sky. "He's a love-sucking demon. He lives here with Damien. Bonbon, where the fuck is Damien?"

"A demon?" Belch stepped back. "What the hell

is *it* doing here?"

"Thanks for ratting us out, Sky," Bonbon snarled and then looked at Gorgonzolina. "Come on, sweetie. Let's go get our things. Looks like we're going to be locked up again. Damien is inside the trailer with the rage demon, by the way!" The two demons walked off.

"Guys, I'm sorry!" Sky said to Bonbon and Gorgonzolina. "I don't know what's going on." Sky looked at the three very large men and then at the trailer. "Is someone going to do something?" Damien was probably inside fighting for his life.

They all scratched their heads.

"I can't believe you people." She looked at Willa. "What about you, witch? Can't you help?"

"Guh!" Willa threaded her pink manicured nails through her hair. Were those highlights? "What's there to do, Sky? My powers won't work on such a beast."

Beast. The word clicked in Sky's head. Beast was what Damien called his twin. "Is that what's been living inside Damien this whole time? A rage demon?" Sky asked Willa.

"I don't know," Willa said like she definitely knew.

There was a loud crash inside the RV, followed by a deep roar.

"I'm going in." Sky approached the door and opened it, sticking her head inside. "Damien! Ohmygod."

CHAPTER TWENTY-EIGHT

MF had woken up just a few minutes after drinking from Maxton, hungrier than she'd ever been. Her throat burned, her skin felt cool, and her brain was on fire. She didn't remember feeling this way the first time she turned, but of course, she'd been in a blind rage, panicking and alone that time.

She got up, scratching her head and rubbing her arms. She felt tingly all over, and her skin was supersensitive.

"Maxton?" She checked the bathroom, living room, and kitchen. He wasn't here? Was this some sort of joke?

She sniffed the air, following the scent of fresh evil human, which led her to the closet door. She opened it and found Stewart standing there, still looking like a zombie.

Pinned to his shirt was a note:

MF, I saw an urgent message from Damien on your shiny rectangle, asking for your help. You were not ready to wake, so I have gone to assist him. I left you this large snack. Please be sure

to save me a bite. I will return shortly. —
Maxton

MF looked at the note again. She then went to the living room and grabbed her phone. Yep, there was an urgent text from Damien, saying to come to his house right away.

"Something's not right." Damien never signed off on his texts. And he certainly didn't do it with the name "D-Dawg."

She looked back toward the closet, her scorched throat screaming for relief. She needed to drink. "No, Maxton needs me more."

She quickly dressed in her black leather pants, biker boots, and leather jacket. She grabbed her keys and bolted to her car, hitting the road like a bat out of hell. But, obviously, not a bat. A brand-spanking-new vampire with a bloodlust that could quickly turn into a crime scene if she didn't hurry.

∂∘ ∘∂

MF pulled up to Damien's two-story mansion, which looked like a war zone with smoke, flashing lights, and water cannons. Police, several ambulances, and firetrucks circled the place. People were running away, screaming as fireballs launched from the upstairs windows, hitting the street.

"Mother of all the fucks. What's going on?" MF pulled over and got out.

Boom!

Boom!

Cruuunch!

It sounded like someone was inside Damien's house, lobbing grenades and crushing walls. Emergency crews were taking cover behind their vehicles.

"Ma'am, you need to get in your car and go," said an officer. "There is a terrorist cell inside. The bomb squad is on the way."

"The guy makes suits. There aren't any terrorists in there." *Unless you count the otherworldly creatures who may or may not be from hell.*

"Ma'am, I said turn around and go."

MF was about to drive away and find a side street to park on so she could sneak around back, but then she remembered something. *I'm a fucking vampire! Woo-hoo!*

"Hey, sir?" MF said. "I think there's a piece of shrapnel in my eye. Can you take a look?"

He leaned in, squinting at her face.

She resisted the urge to chomp on him, but luckily, he smelled bad—as in, he was good. Not so tasty.

"Hello, nice man," she said, hypnotizing him with her eyes. "You are going to walk me to that house. Tell everyone I'm here from…TPD, the Terrorist Peace Department." Sounded like it could be a thing, right? The government had all sorts of cash-sucking useless departments these days. "Nod if you understand."

He nodded.

"Great! Let's go." She marched toward the front of Damien's modern-day palace with a breathtaking view of the glittering cityscape below. Once she got to the porch, she sent the officer away and put her hair up in a bun to protect it from the flames inside.

She leaned through the busted doorjamb. "Hello?" Where the hell were Maxton and Damien? Where was the posse? "Bonbon! Gorg! Pet! Are you here?"

Pet appeared drenched in sweat. "MF! You look very sexy as a vampire. May I stroke your fangs?"

"Pet, what the hell is happening?" MF pointed at the ball of fire just off the foyer.

"Oh, that. Cimil accidentally let a rage demon loose. She was supposed to put it in a new body, but it got away. Maxton is fighting it now. Not winning, by the way."

MF should've known this had something to do with Cimil. That goddess was out of control!

"Um, sorry. But what the hell is a rage demon? Never mind." Maybe it was better just to go and find out for herself. Probably not the brightest idea, given the state of the home, but Maxton was in here. She couldn't lose him now!

MF entered the living room, which was demolished—every piece of furniture overturned and in flames, walls caved in, and parts of the ceiling missing, exposing the upstairs rooms. "Jesus."

"Back it into that corner!" a man yelled from somewhere in the house.

"Don't let him get away this time!" Maxton roared.

"We can't let him leave!" yelled another guy.

"You come for the fun?" said a sharp female voice behind MF.

She turned her head to find Willa standing amongst the rubble near the kitchen, sipping a martini.

"What are you doing here?" MF asked.

"Waiting."

"For?" MF asked.

"To finish my drink. Obviously. Duh…"

MF so wanted to snack on this bitch, but Willa wasn't hers to end. That was—hopefully—Damien's job. "I don't know what he sees in you, but you're definitely a waste of power."

MF flipped up the collar on her leather jacket to protect her neck, cheeks, and ears and charged through the flames toward the voices into the formal dining area.

She skidded to a halt. *Oh boy. I was* not *expecting this.*

Sky was in dirty lavender sweats, sitting on the floor and clinging to Damien's head as he lay unconscious. Two men, both seven feet tall with turquoise eyes, were bloody and singed and trying to corral something bright red in the corner.

One of the men, the one with long black hair, was yelling, "Let's hug it out, bro!"

The other, who wore white underpants, was

chugging Damien's favorite whisky straight from the bottle.

Maxton stood at the center of the room, a predatory look in his dark eyes. His new suit was smoldering and in tatters.

MF tried to focus on the rage demon, but it kept darting side to side like a big bouncing fireball.

"Come on. Stop being such a coward. Fight me, beast!" Maxton yelled.

Oh crap! That's Damien's beast! MF recognized that smell anywhere.

A few weeks ago, she'd "met" the beast when he took over Damien's body during a dinner party. MF had been speechless and frozen in the middle of the slaughter, as guests attempted to run. She would've run, too, except that she'd been a predator herself once. She knew not to flee. It only provoked an attack.

When it was all over, everyone was dead, and Damien just...snapped back. That night, MF tried to wash the smell of bloodshed from her hair, but the scent stuck for days.

Sulphur.

Rotting flesh.

Almonds.

The scent of hell. It was the same smell in the air right now. That moving fireball had to be the beast.

A rage demon, huh? She'd never heard of them, but it totally made sense.

The beast launched a fireball at Maxton, who

barely got out of the way in time. The ball exploded on the wall. MF used her arms to shield her head from the sparks.

I have to help take this thing down. "Maxton!" MF yelled.

Maxton's head swiveled in her direction. His green eyes lit up. "Wow. Just…wow."

"What?" she snapped.

"I never imagined how hot you'd look undead."

MF bowed her head. "Thank you, sir. And ditto."

"What is a ditto?" Maxton asked.

"Never mind. Let's cage this fucker." She paused. "How do we cage it?"

The man with long black hair stepped forward, fists clenched. "You must look into its heart and find love." He shook his head. "Fuck. I hate this power. It's bullshit!" He looked at Maxton and MF. "You squeeze it until its heart pops out. And do it fast. Because if it escapes, it *will* multiply or, worse, reopen the portals to the demon world."

"You go left," Maxton said to MF, "and I'll go right."

"I will block the door," said the black-haired man.

The guy in his underwear was still working on the scotch.

Cimil appeared out of nowhere, waving her arms in the air. "Whoa. Whoa. Whoa! Hold up, Votan." She was addressing the guy with black hair.

MF and Maxton exchanged confused glances.

"Cimil," snarled Votan, "move. I will deal with you later. In a loving way," he added. "Dammit! That is not what I meant."

"I can subdue the beast," Cimil said, "but want something in return."

"Here we go again," Votan said. "You always create the crisis and then come in to save the day, but only if you get something in return."

"So?" Cimil said.

Damien was back on his feet, blinking rapidly like he was recovering from a bad knock on the head. Meanwhile, the rage demon was attempting to bust through the wall.

"It's over, Cimil," Damien said, pushing Sky behind him protectively. One side of her blonde hair had been singed off. "You let it loose. You did this. And I am going to end it."

"No. No. No. I want a war! I want death. And I shall have it!" Cimil yelled.

Everyone except the demon froze. The demon jumped up and down. "War! War! War!"

Strange. MF still couldn't make out what the bugger looked like.

The guy in white underwear shook his head. "It's your damned powers, Votan. Cimil can't handle them. She cannot be the God of Death and War."

"I'm realizing that," Votan said. "But how do we switch it?"

"We have to set everything back the way it was!" Cimil spouted. "That's what I was trying to do. We must get our powers back the way they were, which means we all go through a demon portal again."

So that had been Cimil's grand plan all along?

"The demon portals are closed. For good," Votan argued.

"He," she pointed to the rage demon, "can reopen it, but we have to give him something he wants. His own human shell so he can experience the pleasures of the physical world."

MF and Maxton exchanged glances. She couldn't speak for him, but she felt like they'd walked into the middle of a supernatural soap opera.

Cimil went on, "And as I'm sure you can all appreciate, if we open that portal, the demon issue will return, which is why we will need help to keep them in check. Vampires, weres, chupacabras. And yes, us gods. We must bring everyone back."

MF noticed the demon stopped moving for a split second. The thing was the size of a hamster. Kind of looked like one, too, but without hair. It was almost…cute. *That's it? That's the rage demon kicking the crap out of everyone?*

"Maxton!" She pounced on the thing, and Maxton grabbed its body, squeezing until he heard a *pop!*

A red Jell-O like substance went everywhere, covering them, the room, and everyone in it.

Ew. All this mess, and it didn't even have a real body? *Demons are weird.*

"No!" Cimil screamed. "No! What have you done?" Cimil fell to the floor, bawling. "He was our only chance to get our old powers back. What have you done?"

"I think she foiled another one of your idiotic plans." Damien flashed a smile at MF. "Good job, MF. Hey, you…look different."

MF and Maxton stood up, and she flashed her shiny new fangs.

"Ah, very nice." Damien turned to Sky, brushing her non-charred hair from her face. "Are you all right?"

"Yes, can we get out of here?" Sky asked.

"Probably for the best since the authorities outside now believe I'm running a terrorist cell with sloppy bomb-making skills."

"Maxton and I can help with that." MF smiled at Maxton. Maybe she could find a little snack outside, too.

"What the fuck?" Willa appeared in the doorway and dropped her martini glass. "Where's the beast?"

"Dead," said Votan.

Willa looked at Cimil, who was still crumpled in a ball on the floor. "We had a deal, Cimil!"

"Yes, and you idiots fucked it all up." Cimil sobbed. "Maxton was supposed to make an army of vampires and turn my hubby, who would lead our new army. The beast was going to reopen the portal so I could get my old powers back. The gods were supposed to see what a mess everything was and come out of retirement. It was going to be perfect again."

"What about me?" Willa growled. "What about our deal?"

"You die either way," Cimil said.

Willa looked stunned.

"Don't be so shocked." Cimil flung a hand through the air. "You tormented the poor tailor his entire life. He only loved you because of your handy whammy."

"Is it true, Willa?" Damien said. "Did you bespell me?"

"Oh shite." Willa turned and started running. Damien was about to go after her, but Sky grabbed his hand. "Let her go, Damien. She's not worth it."

"Cimil, you are coming with us," Votan said.

Cimil looked up, snot flowing from her nose. "No. I won't be locked up. Roberto won't allow it."

"It was his suggestion right before he left. Oh, and he told me to make sure you know you're no longer welcome. He doesn't want to be a vampire anymore. Neither do your children."

Oh god. MF suddenly realized that the list Cimil had given Maxton wasn't exactly a list of willing participants. He would have had to turn some against their will.

MF looked proudly at Maxton. He'd made the right choice. He was a good man.

"We'd better hurry up and leave before the

bomb squad arrives," said Votan.

Votan and Belch dragged Cimil out the back. Damien and Sky followed.

Maxton gazed hungrily at MF. "You look lovely all covered in demon blood, by the way. Would you care for a quickie? We can find a room upstairs that is uncharred before we go outside and erase everyone's memories?"

Oh yes. She would like that very much.

CHAPTER TWENTY-NINE

Damien and Sky hosed off the demon goop out back and then made their way to a hotel for the night to take proper showers.

"So, how does it feel?" Sky asked, sitting on the edge of the bed in a robe. "Your twin is gone."

"Like there is a hollow space inside. But pleasant." He actually felt lighter. "I never knew he was a demon. Everyone in my family believed we Greystone males simply lived with a wicked twin inside." Clearly, they'd been deceived. Why? And by whom? He would find out eventually.

"How did Cimil get the thing out of you?" Sky asked.

"She had a chamber of sorts. I am guessing it is what SBP uses in the process of removing one's soul to implant it into a new body like the one you have."

Speaking of bodies. Damien stared at Sky's lovely new face. She truly was gorgeous, no matter the body. Though, her blonde hair might need a trim. It was significantly shorter on one side.

She locked eyes with him, and his heart began accelerating. He felt like he'd been waiting forever for her.

"Damien, there's something I need to tell you." She sighed. "I love you. And I always will."

His inside felt heavy suddenly. He could tell by her tone she was about to drop a bomb. "But?"

"But I made a promise to myself to follow through on this whole SBP thing. I am going to stop them from the inside, like you suggested."

"Well, this is great. I completely support it." And he loved that she wasn't turning her back on her morals.

"No," she shook her head, "you don't understand. This could take a long time, and I can't risk getting the people I love involved in all this stuff again. I have a chance right now to go in with a clean slate. New identity. No ties to any of you. You'll all be safe no matter what happens to me."

"Are you…leaving?"

"Will you please look in on Amelia and Miguel? Your beast is gone, so you're not a threat anymore."

"Sky, you can't do this. I chose you. I love you." Strange to say it and not fear horrible repercussions.

Sky locked eyes with him again. "I'm sorry, Damien. But I know you of all people should understand."

He did. And he didn't. He'd been pushing away the world for centuries in an attempt to keep them all safe. Now, he was beginning to realize how much he'd missed out on. He'd wasted so much of his life feeling guilty for having loved Willa and for the events their love triggered. None of it had been real. Not the love anyway. Now he'd finally met a woman he wanted to share his life with, but she was about to leave him?

Out of love. Just as he had done. Damien laughed.

"What's so funny?" Sky asked.

"Cimil. I think this was part of her plan, too. She knew I did not want to serve her, and I think she knew you were the reason I'd keep fighting to get out from under her thumb. That reason is gone now." What if this whole thing, SBP and Sky's determination to stop them, had been set up by Cimil? It was very possible given everything he'd seen.

"Doesn't matter now," Sky said. "Because you're free. By the way, where are the demons and Pet?"

"I saw them sneaking away while Votan and Belch were fighting the beast. I suspect Bonbon and Gorgonzolina didn't want to be locked away again." Demons were prohibited in the human world. In fact, that was how this whole thing had started with Cimil. She'd discovered he was harboring Bonbon and demanded a favor in return for her silence. That favor had led to him meeting Sky. "Pet probably went with them to find new objects to grind on."

"So you really are free. Just like you wanted all

along."

Damien nodded solemnly. Perhaps loving Sky was a mistake. Not because she wasn't worthy, but because he was not destined to find happiness. *Not in the cards for me.*

"Damien, I am going to leave now. I'll catch a ride to my sister's motel and say goodbye to them in the morning." She stood.

"Are you sure you'll be okay? You're wearing a robe."

"Not the weirdest outfit I've ever seen in LA."

True.

He stood and walked over to her, gazing down into her stunning green eyes. He could still see Sky in there—her fearlessness, her lively spark, her good nature.

He bent his head down and kissed her, savoring the feel of her in his arms.

She broke away. "I love you."

He nodded and watched her go. He felt himself breaking inside.

CHAPTER THIRTY

MF and Maxton returned to her apartment just before dawn. It had taken hours to tell all of the emergency crews that they had not seen demon fireballs, that there were no terrorists living in the house, and that it was a simple case of a hot-water heater gone bad. Oh, and the owner wasn't home and that wasn't blood all over the dining room. Red paint. With chunks of meat. No biggie.

"I'm so hungry, Maxton." MF plopped on her bed, too tired to care that she still had demon blood on her.

Maxton lay down next to her. "It was a fine evening though. Lovemaking, turning you, fighting that beast, more lovemaking. A very good time."

MF chuckled. Maxton had looked completely in his element. "You're going to have to teach me to fight like you. You're a badass."

"Thank you. I have always wanted to be a naughty donkey." He rolled toward her, staring deeply into her eyes. "I must return to the jungle."

Her cold heart skipped a beat. What? He was

leaving her? "I thought you said you were going to stay?"

"I will return. I must retrieve my parrot. And my gold."

"What parrot?"

"He's the sixth generation to stay with me."

MF wanted to laugh. "So all this time, you weren't really alone."

"I would not say that."

"Can I come with you?" She held her breath, hoping he'd finally say yes.

"I would like that."

She smiled, her new vampire heart beating warmly. She'd just have to talk to Damien first and let him know. Of course, he had Sky now, and those two lovebirds were probably getting busy.

"What do you want to do about Stewart?" she asked.

"You do not want to eat him?"

"I don't know. The thought of having his blood inside me makes me feel kinda icky. It'll be like I'm carrying around the murderer of my family in my veins."

Maxton nodded. "We don't have to eat him. We could just kill the bastard."

"But doesn't that feel too easy? I mean, we have to live an eternity missing our families. He took them from us. Why shouldn't he live out the rest of his natural life suffering too?"

"You make a very good point. What did you

have in mind?"

"Someone needs to help look after the shop while I'm away with you. Why not make him do it." Not that Stewart could sew, but he could do inventory, organize the stockroom, and ring up customers. She could instruct him to simply follow Damien's instructions like a good little human.

"As you wish. Now take off your clothes. I want to see your strange land strip again. It is very sexy."

"Landing strip. It means—"

He started peeling down her leather pants.

"Never mind!"

∂ ∞

Five days later, MF and Maxton were back in the jungle. She'd texted Damien before leaving, letting him know she'd be gone a while but had left a surprise in the storeroom.

A helper. Be sure to feed and water him. Give hugs to the demons and Pet. Sky, too.

Funny, how they were all from different worlds but felt like family. Damien the stubborn father figure always trying to protect everyone. Bonbon and Gorgonzolina were like a clueless aunt and uncle, stuck in their own little world. Pet was the out-of-control teen with a sexual appetite that made her do stupid shit all the time. MF wondered what that made her.

Definitely the cool older sister.

And now they'd have Sky. Would she be like their mother, looking after everyone, being a source of strength and encouragement? And of course, Maxton. *Can't forget about him.*

If I'm the cool sister, that makes Maxton my cool boyfriend. Of course, they were much more than that. Maxton had already started hinting at marriage once he completed his confessions. Could take a few years to get through his list of sins, but whatever. They had all the time in the world now. *Vampires, baby! Yeah!*

"All right. This is all of it." Maxton emerged from his cave, holding a huge sack.

"What is that?"

"My gold, some books, and the remnants of Damien's suit."

"I think you can leave the rags behind. I'll make you a new one," she said.

"It has sentimental value."

"You really love your suits, don't you?" He'd hung on to that other one for a few hundred years.

"To me, they are reminder: Though I am a vampire, I am not an animal. I am a gentleman, and I alone control my life."

"Not quite *alone* anymore. But, yeah, a reminder to be our best self is a good thing. Especially because your days of turning people inside out are over."

"That wasn't me."

Huh? "Then whose are those?" She eyed the desiccated inside-out bodies hanging from a nearby tree.

"Those are my parrot's decorations, meant to keep people away."

She crinkled her nose. *What a morbid bird. Strong, too.* "So where's he?"

"Oh, yes. I almost forgot." Maxton whistled. Suddenly, the trees began to rustle. The ground shook beneath her feet.

"What the hell is that?" she asked, taking two steps back.

"That's Parrot." The bushes beside them were suddenly flat, like something large and invisible stood on top of them.

"Maxton! What is that?" she repeated.

"I told you. It is Parrot, my hellhound. Don't worry. He doesn't eat much."

Hellhound? Was that why the ground always shook around here? How fucking big was it?

"Wo-wow," she stuttered nervously. "You are-are full of surprises, Maxton." MF had never seen a hellhound, nor wanted to, and now she knew she never would. They were invisible. "But you can't take a hellhound to LA."

"I cannot leave him here. He has guarded my lair for years."

So Maxton hadn't been doing all that killing? It sort of relieved her. He wasn't exactly a saint; maybe his road to redemption wasn't as bad as he thought.

Maxton stepped in front of her, gazing down

with his jungle green eyes. MF inhaled deeply, losing herself in his beauty.

"From the first moment I met you," he said, "I knew you were special. Your presence soothed my soul."

It did? "Then why did you push me away?"

"A bad man like me," he shrugged, "has no right to be with someone like you, MF. You are too good." He cupped her cheek and kissed her deeply. Her heart melted as his mouth moved with hers.

He suddenly pulled away, staring with those hypnotic eyes. "Thank you for giving me a new life and new purpose. I love you, Mountain Flower."

Her heart soared. "I love you, too." They really were happy together. Strange because it was just as Cimil promised. *A vampire. A family. A purpose.* MF had all three now. It almost made her feel guilty that Cimil was locked up in some Uchben prison for immortals.

"Okay," MF sighed contently, "you can bring the hellhound." What was one more member of the posse, right?

"Do not worry," Maxton said cheerfully. "He is very docile. Mostly. Come, Parrot." Maxton started marching down the hill.

She felt a hot breath on the back of her neck. "Oh fuck. Oh fuck." She chased down after Maxton.

"Are you sure Brutus is going to let that thing on the plane back to LA?"

"Who says we must tell him?"

CHAPTER THIRTY-ONE

Damien opened up the shop, feeling a little sprier than he had this past week. He missed Sky but kept telling himself that as long as she was alive, their story wasn't over. He would see her again someday soon, and if it was meant to be, she would stay. As his wife.

In the meantime, he had a house to rebuild. He couldn't very well propose to Sky when this was all over and not have a home to offer her.

Alone at last in my shop! As it was always meant to be. Just a man and his suits. No more frilly dresses and circus animals.

He walked into the storeroom and switched on the lights. *Almost alone.* "Good morning, Stewart. I got you coffee and a doughnut. You may use the bathroom to relieve yourself and clean up."

Damien gave it some thought. He knew this was the man who murdered MF's family, but he really wanted things to go back the way they were before at Greystone and Sons. Minus the rage demon.

No pesky fairies, Chihuahuas licking their genitals

in front of customers, ex-vampires with poor fashion choices, or gods manipulating me into doing their evil bidding. Life was finally looking up.

"Stewart, after you have cleaned up," Damien said, "I think I am going to cut you free. I will get you a bus ticket back to Tijuana."

"Thank you," Stewart said in a drab voice.

"But once you get home, you are not to run. Do you understand? MF gets to decide what to do with you." Who knew what she had planned, but it wasn't Damien's concern.

Damien put on some music, unlocked the register, and started counting out the bills. The bell above the door chimed.

He looked up, but there was no one. An ice-cold breeze wafted through the store, pushing clothes aside.

Damien swallowed down a cold lump in his throat. "Hello?"

Suddenly, the door chimed again. In sauntered Bonbon and Gorgonzolina with Pet riding on her head.

"Hey, man. Wussup," said Bonbon.

"I told you to stop allowing Pet to be seen in public. What are you doing here?" Damien asked.

"We got a text, telling us to come."

"Bonbon, you don't own a phone," Damien pointed out.

Bonbon looked up at the ceiling. "That was you, Sky? Hey, lookin' great, by the way. I wasn't into your new body. No ass."

Damien's blood pressure hit the floor. "Sky?"

"She says she's dead again." Pet swirled around in a circle.

MF waltzed in with Maxton behind her.

"Hey, guys!" she said. "We just got back and saw the text. What's the emergency?"

Pet fluttered to the center of the room. "Sky says she was murdered. Again. And SBP took Amelia and Miguel—for test subjects."

"Oh no," said MF. "You're dead again, Sky?"

"Don't you worry, Sky," said Bonbon, "we are going to get your family back."

"And Maxton's Parrot will make them pay," MF snarled.

Damien blinked. "This can't fucking be happening."

↷ ↶

From her jail cell in the Uchben maximum-security prison, Cimil flipped through her *Sunset Magazine*, dog-earing the pages with horrible designs so she wouldn't forget to punish the designers in the afterlife.

"Ew. Gold plating? You're definitely going to hell." A small gust of wind whipped through the air. "Oh, hi, Minky," Cimil whispered.

She listened to the latest report.

"Oh, that is too bad. Sky's a ghost again." Cimil

shrugged. "Well, we all have a part to play. But no one still suspects a thing?"

Minky shook her head no.

"This is great." Funny, though. Not one person stopped to really think about why she'd made sure everyone showed up at the same time to fight that rage demon. Everyone except her sweet Roberto, who only needed to see it.

"Soon, the rest of the pieces will fall into place, Minky. You'll see. It's going to be the biggest shit show ever."

Cimil listened.

"Of course I have a backup plan. But really, what could possibly go wrong?"

TO BE CONTINUED...

Click here for updates on book #3, coming 2024!

www.mimijean.net/books/immortal-tailor-book-3

OR

Keep reading to score a FREE *Vampire in the Jungle* signed bookmark!

AUTHOR'S NOTE

Hello to all my Immortal Tailor fans!

I hope you enjoyed Maxton and MF's story, served with a heaping helping of Damien's crazy life! Now, with even more posse goodness! Haha... Two love-sucking demons, two vampires, a sex-fairy, a hellhound, and a ghost. Oh boy!

Just to keep everyone on track, we still don't know what the fallout will be from the Russian mob massacre (book 1) or who's really behind SBP. Is it the evil California governor Newberry or someone else?

And where exactly is K'ak? Wasn't he supposed to be looking after things for the gods?

Also, now that Sky is back in her ghost body, what does that mean for her and Damien? Because Willa isn't dead, and I don't think she's truly out of Damien's life.

More importantly, I wonder how things will change for Damien now that he doesn't have a rage demon inside him. It could make him more vulnerable to his enemies. Or…it might force him to step up and become the deadly, violent man he left behind.

We shall see!

I plan to release book 3 in mid-2024. Be sure to sign up to my very non-spammy newsletter for updates by going to www.mimijean.net or clicking here: SIGN UP!

Now on to the good stuff!

If you'd like **a FREE signed *Vampire in the Jungle* bookmark,** just follow the steps below.

International okay!

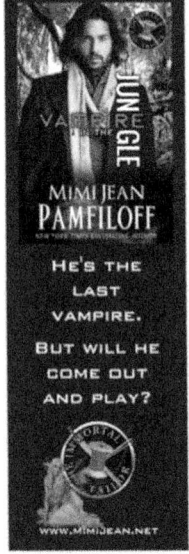

STEP ONE: Email me at Mimi@mimijean.net

STEP TWO: Provide your complete shipping info (include the country if you're outside the US).

STEP THREE: If you wrote a review for *Vampire in the Jungle*, THANK YOU for supporting me! Be sure to provide a link or screenshot. If you're first in line, I will include a magnet. It's first ask, first get, and I do run out! But, as always, you will get a big THANK YOU from me.

STEP FOUR: Give me about 3–4 weeks. I'm pretty slow at getting mail out, but I do get to it. I send email confirmations once they go.

Thank you for reading my crazy stories for over ten years!

WITH LOVE,
Mimi

ACKNOWLEDGMENTS

Thank you to all the wonderful people who work so hard and pitch in so I can continue bringing these banana stories to my readers! Jaycee at Sweet 'N Spicy Designs, LD (best PA ever), Kylie Gilmore, Pauline Nolet, Paul Salvette, and Stephanie Elliot.

To my family, thank you for still putting up with me and my crazy work life. I love you guys.

To my readers, ten years you've been reading my work. That makes you as crazy as I am! Love it. And thank you from the bottom of my heart.

With Love,
Mimi Jean

WANT TO KEEP TRACK OF YOUR MJP READS?

Check out my reading lists!

Mimi Jean Pamfiloff
PARANORMAL

ACCIDENTALLY YOURS

Standalone, humorous

MERMEN

Dark Fantasy
Not standalone

IMMORTAL MATCHMAKERS

Standalone, humorous. Accidentally Yours spinoff

MR. ROOK'S ISLAND

Dark Fantasy
Not standalone

KING'S

Dark Fantasy.
Standalone; Mack

THE LIBRARIAN'S VAMPIRE ASSISTANT

Cozy Mysteries.
Standalone: Vampire Man & Fanged Love

WALL MEN

Dark Fantasy
Not standalone

REVOLUVTION

WIP. Fantasy
Not standalone

THE IMMORTAL TAILOR

WIP.
Paranormal

CONTEMPORARY

OHELLNO

Standalone, rom-com

HAPPY PANTS

Standalone, rom-com

THE BOYFRIEND COLLECTOR

Contemporary
Duet

FATE BOOK

New Adult
Duet

FUGLY

Contemporary
Duet

WISH

Contemporary
Standalone

M.O. MACK

Standalone Thrillers

LOOKING FOR MORE SUPERNATURAL FUN?

The complete *Wall Men Trilogy* is available NOW!

MONSTERS? VAMPIRES? GHOSTS AND DEMONS? MEN WHO GUARD THE WALL BETWEEN US AND THEM.

I'm sitting at my grandma's bedside, moments away from losing her, when she begins to rant about monsters and men trapped in her old mansion. I practically grew up there, so I know it's the pain meds talking. There's nothing inside that drafty house except rotting books, rusty pipes, and neglected antiques.

"I've written down all the rules, Lake. You must follow them," she tells me, gasping for air. "The Wall Men cannot get free. They are soulless and evil. They will try to seduce you. But you cannot listen. They must remain chained to the wall."

What the…?

In her final breath, she makes me swear to read her journals. But above all, I must promise to never go inside her bedroom, the one that's always kept locked.

Madness!

Weeks after her funeral, I'm forced to confront the neglected estate she's left behind. I can't afford the taxes, so it has to be cleaned and sold.

That's when I hear a deep velvety voice on the other side of her bedroom door, demanding to be let out.

And dammit if I don't want to break my promise and see who's on the other side.

CHAPTER ONE

"Are you sure she doesn't have more time?" I clutch a bouquet of yellow roses to my chest, whispering to the hospice nurse in the hallway. I pray there's been a mistake. I'm not ready to lose my grandma, even though I've known for months she's nearing the end.

"I'm sorry, Lake, I wish we could do more." She offers a sympathetic look that feels rehearsed. Of course, I know it's her job to help families deal with the inevitable, so I'm not put off.

I appreciate her professionalism at a time when

my heart is breaking. I thought Grandma Rain had a few more weeks, but as I was driving over just now, I got the call. This will be my last chance to speak to her.

I hold back the tears. "Thank you for taking such good care of her."

"I'm here for you. Whatever you need." The nurse gently squeezes my shoulder. "I've given your grandmother a sedative to keep her comfortable, so she might be a little out of it. Press the red button if you need anything."

I thank the nurse again and enter the white sterile room. The blinds are open, and the afternoon sun is shining across the foot of Grandma's bed. They've taken off her oxygen and unhooked her IV. It was one of her final requests. No crap attached to her body.

"Grandma Rain? I'm here."

She doesn't respond, but her chest is moving beneath her favorite gray flannel nightgown.

I tug on the beige blanket covering her frail legs and bring it up to her waist. I don't know how to digest the harshness of the moment. I don't know how to say goodbye. Grandma Rain raised me as her own after my parents disappeared. Still, there's a part of me that feels grateful her suffering is coming to an end. Pancreatic cancer is not a nice way to go.

"Grandma Rain, can you hear me? I've come to say goodbye."

She doesn't respond, and I can only hope she

knows I'm here. She's not dying alone.

I grab the green pleather armchair from the corner of the small room and drag it across the linoleum floor, parking it next to her bed.

I sit and take her cool soft hand. So many thoughts are running through my mind. If she can hear me, what do I say? I want to thank her for everything. I want her to know how much I love her and—

"You're late," she snaps, cracking open a pale blue eye.

I jolt in my seat. "Oh my God. You're awake."

"What took you so long to get here, girl? Who makes an old woman wait to die?"

"I'm—I'm so sorry. Jim made me stay an extra hour." Jim is my boss at the 911 call center. We're always shorthanded. Mostly because the pay is shit, the hours are long, and the job can be stressful. It was only supposed to be a temporary gig while I looked for a teaching job, but that's life. I needed a job close to home.

The good thing about Tionesta, Pennsylvania, where I work, is that it's generally quiet. We get the tourists in the summer who go up to the lake and sometimes drink too much—boating accidents and heatstroke—but that's about the worst of it. We actually live about thirty minutes east of Tionesta in Mayburg. Population: It depends. Mayburg is literally a bend in the Tionesta Creek along Route 666 near the Allegheny National Forest. There are a few family farms, but most of it's thick wooded forest. Cold as hell in the winter.

"Your boss is a useless fuckhole," Grandma Rain says. "Someone should light his dick on fire and throw him off a cliff before he procreates."

Did I mention that Grandma Rain is a foul-mouthed curmudgeon who hates just about everyone except me, her dog Master, and her live-in handyman, Bardolf?

I'm told by Bardolf, "Bard," that when Mom was around, she and Grandma didn't get along either. "Like two feral cats, ready to scratch each other's eyes out," he once said. Dad was barely welcome on Grandma's estate. It was why the police accused Grandma of killing my parents when they disappeared over twenty years ago. I was almost nine at the time.

Obviously, no evidence was ever found, but the rumors never stopped. The locals hate Grandma just as much as she hates them.

As for me, I don't know what I'm going to do after she's gone. Grandma Rain and I are opposites in every sense of the word—she's mean, I'm not. She's tall, I'm five two. She wears her hair short, mine is long and dark. Blue eyes, brown eyes. Winter, summer. Hates everyone, loves everyone. Still, despite our differences, we always got along.

Maybe because I grew up feeling lucky to have her. She loved me, encouraged me to be independ-ent, and made sure I got an education. I never minded her eccentricities or profanity because deep down she's the sort of woman who'll fight tooth and nail for you. And for the record, she loved my mom, Storm. Her disappearance is what made Grandma so inconsolably bitter, though she'd never admit it. Too prideful.

"I'll be sure to let my boss know you were thinking of him." I'll leave out the part about him being a useless fuckhole or lighting his dick on fire.

"And," Grandma Rain adds, "you be sure to read that speech at my funeral. Word for word. No sugarcoating. I want those pieces of shit to know how little their lives mean."

Doubt anyone could miss the meaning. The speech literally says, *You're all useless pieces of shit. Rot in hell.*

I want to roll my eyes. How's it possible to be filled with so much hate in one's final moments? Also, she and I both know that no one from town is going to her funeral.

"Shouldn't you be thinking about things that make you happy, Grandma? Your garden? Master? All your books?" *Me?*

"You think I've been hanging on for hours just to take a piss down memory lane? Get your head out of your ass, child. I've got something important to say, so you listen and listen good. From this day forward, there is no place in your life for happy thoughts. Put it out of your stupid head." She grabs my wrist, digging her nails into my skin.

"Ow. What are you doing? Let go." I try to pull away, but she digs in harder.

The nurse said she'd be out of it, but Grandma Rain seems disturbingly lucid, her pale blue eyes intense.

"Lake, I broke the rules. Once and only once. It cost me your mother's life. Your father's, too. Not that I gave a crap about him. Useless prick. But you loved that man. And you lost him because of me."

Outside, the sun is suddenly eclipsed by a dark cloud, casting a gray shadow over the room. The air around us instantly chills, and the fine hairs on the back of my neck stiffen.

"Are you saying you had something to do with their disappearance?"

"I had *everything* to do with it," she spits. "I turned my back on the rules for one minute, and the Wall Men took them. They did it to punish me because I wouldn't set them free."

What the…?

My horror turns to deep sadness as I realize she's fallen into a delusional state. Grandma Rain has always marched to her own beat—hanging lavender sachets over doors, lighting massive sage bonfires on the front lawn during full moons, and planting quartz crystals all over the property. But this is different. This is crazy talk.

I pry her hand off my wrist. "Just try to relax, okay? I'll call the nurse." I reach for the cord with the button by her side.

"No!" She smacks my hand away.

"Grandma! You can't hit—"

"You must hear what I have to say, Lake. You *must* listen. The monsters on the other side of my bedroom wall are *nothing* like in the fairy tales. They will strip the flesh from your bones, slice by slice. They will drain your blood to fill their goblets. They will rape you, rip the child from your swollen belly, and eat it while you watch." Her voice lowers to a chilled whisper, her eyelids twitching with emotion. "They don't just want to end us, Lake. They want to hurt us first. They want to watch humans scream."

I cover my mouth. I don't know how to process the disgusting thoughts coming from her mouth. I get that she's not of sound mind, but where is all this coming from?

"Stop, Grandma, just stop," I say in a firm but calm tone. "I don't want to hear any more."

"Foolish girl. I'm trying to tell you something. The only thing protecting the wall between us and the pain are the Wall Men. The monsters fear them because they are a thousand times more vicious than anything else. Which is why you must *never* unchain them from the wall. Do you understand? You must never give in. They will use threats. They will use your fear against you, and if that fails, they will try to seduce you."

Seduce? What the hell?

She continues, "But they are violent, soulless

men, Lake. They only feel hunger—for bloodshed, fucking, food. It is their hunger that feeds their blind rage and keeps us safe. Never forget that. And above all, girl, you keep that damned bedroom door closed. Do not go inside. It is too dangerous." She points a shaky finger in my face. "Promise me you'll read my journals. All the rules are there. I've left them for you in my office."

"Grandma, I—"

"Promise!"

"Okay, I promise." I know she's dying and on meds, but I'm suddenly realizing her words are not the result of either. *She's disturbed.* Grandma Rain has always kept the master bedroom door locked. She's never stayed in there once that I'm aware of. Always slept on the couch in her study.

So this is why? All these years, she believed there were men chained to the wall inside, guarding us from monsters?

My heart sinks into a deep hole, comprehending that she's been mentally ill for years, and I did nothing to help her. How did I not see the signs? How could I have sat by, chalking up her extreme behavior to a textbook case of eccentricity?

I swallow hard, a wave of guilt steamrolling over me. *I did nothing to help her. Nothing.*

Grandma gasps and clutches her chest, sputtering out her words, "Hide my journals in a safe place after you read them. And if you fuck up, burn down the house. It will buy everyone time to hide." She closes her eyes.

"Grandma Rain?" I grip her shoulder and give it a shake, but she doesn't respond. "Grandma, wake up." The tears pool in my eyes. "Grandma!"

Like a switch has flipped, I watch the muscles in her face relax. All signs of life evaporate like a wisp of steam.

This can't be happening. She can't be gone.

A bolt of lightning strikes just outside the window, and thunder explodes, rattling everything in the room. The ground tremors beneath my feet.

Holy shit. Was that an earthquake?

My gaze slowly returns to the face I've known my entire life, and suddenly, I don't recognize it. Grandma Rain is at peace. And one thing everyone knows? She was never at peace.

"Goodbye. I love you."

FOR MORE, GO TO:

www.mimijean.net/wallmen1

ABOUT THE AUTHOR

MIMI JEAN PAMFILOFF is a *New York Times* bestselling author who writes insane plot twists that will have you burning through the pages. Whether it's Romance, Suspense/Thriller, or Fantasy, there are always big heroes to root for, smart and re-sourceful heroines, and a ton of heart-pumping excitement in every story.

Mimi lives with her extremely patient husband ("Be right there! Just one more page, honey!"), two pirates-in-training (their boys), and their three spunky dragons (really, just very tiny dogs with big attitudes) Snowy, Mini, and Mack, in the vampire-unfriendly state of Arizona.

Sign up for Mimi's mailing list for giveaways and
new release news!

STALK MIMI:
www.mimijean.net
pinterest.com/mimijeanromance
instagram.com/mimijeanpamfiloff
facebook.com/MimiJeanPamfiloff

Printed in Dunstable, United Kingdom